UNBREAKABLE LOVE

RETRIBUTION SERIES
BOOK 3

MORGAN JAMES

ONE

Mia

The quiet click of the door seemed symbolic as I once again walked away from the man I'd thought I loved. It was as if a chapter of my life had closed, the slam of disappointment echoing in my ears. My body warred with my mind, and I felt sick with grief, unable to fathom that I'd made the exact same mistake. It seemed as if every memory, every kiss, every touch had been destined for this moment.

"Mia?"

I turned away and steeled my spine, avoiding those intense green-brown eyes.

"Are you ready?"

Glancing one last time at the solid oak door, I gave a single curt nod. The sooner I was away from this place, the better. My heart ached, my eyes burning with tears I barely managed to hold back. I needed to put distance between myself and Jack once and for all—though I feared that this time, I was too far gone. There might not be any chance of healing now.

Bella bumped against my legs, and I absently reached down to pat the dog's head. A sad smile curved my lips, though the crack in my heart fractured and expanded. The dog only served as a reminder of the man who had hurt me —not once, but twice. A pair of soulful brown eyes stared up at me as if reading my thoughts. It was strange to feel a kinship with the dog because of her owner, but I certainly wasn't going to pass up the silent comfort she offered. When I finally left this godforsaken mountain, I would have to avoid him.

"Bye, Bella." I dropped to one knee and hugged the dog tightly around the neck. Steeling myself, I pushed to my feet and stepped off the porch, head held high. Trudging through the snow, I followed Donahue to the SUV, and he held the door as I began to climb inside.

Bella trailed me like a shadow the whole way, and I gently admonished her as she stood beside my door. "Bella, go home." Still, she stood there watching me like she could see every rioting emotion inside. "Bella..." My voice cracked.

The sheriff's voice drifted toward me, soft and sure. "It's okay. She can come."

He opened the back door, and Bella hopped inside and snuggled up on the backseat. With a shake of his head, the sheriff shut the door, then rounded the car and slid into the driver seat.

Unable to look at the cabin, I closed my eyes. A glutton for punishment, I was terrified that my resolve would waver, and I'd stupidly throw myself from the moving vehicle and back into his arms. When I finally felt the tell-tale bump of the SUV's wheels bouncing onto the road, I turned in the seat and gazed out the window, watching as the landscape zipped by in a white blur. I discreetly lifted a shoulder to brush away an errant tear as it dripped down my chin.

From a few feet away, Donahue cleared his throat. "Can I say something?"

I turned a wry glance on him. "Would it stop you if I said no?"

He chuckled. "Probably not."

I lifted a brow, and he smirked at me before continuing. "I've known Jack for a couple years now, and if there's one thing I know about Prescott, it's that he's a hard-headed bastard. Excuse my French." I snorted in agreement, and his expression sobered. "I don't know exactly what happened, but if it's any consolation at all, I think he really does care for you. He's been trying like hell to figure out who's behind this. He didn't even tell me you were there with him."

My brows drew together. "Doesn't that prove my point?"

"Maybe, maybe not." Donahue paused. "I think he refused to tell anyone you were there because he didn't know who he could trust. He wouldn't have put you in danger by announcing your location, even to me."

The truth of his statement hit me hard, but anger wouldn't allow me to forgive so easily. "He should have told me."

The sheriff held up a hand. "I can't say I disagree. All I'm saying is, maybe he had his reasons."

"It wasn't his decision to make," I retorted bitterly, sinking back in my seat and wrapping my arms around my waist. He'd lied to me, damn it, and I wasn't ready to hear his excuses for doing so. I didn't want to hear his reasons for keeping me a secret—I wasn't ready to admit yet that he might be right.

I closed my eyes and leaned my head against the

window, faces and images flashing through my mind. It all made sense now. I'd felt something when Donahue had spoken of questioning two people—he'd been speaking of Janine and Brent. Mentally replaying the conversation in my mind, I wondered if one or both of them could possibly have been involved. I didn't want to contemplate the possibility.

My head throbbed, and there were still chunks of memory missing. It would probably be a while before everything came back, and all I wanted to do now was go curl up somewhere and cry. I tried to sort out what I remembered. My childhood was plain as day. Dad, Jack, Brent, Janine. I remembered all of them. I remembered the words Jack had thrown at me as if it had happened just yesterday instead of almost nine years ago. I remembered the accident, the fear I'd felt at running from the stranger in my house, the one who caused me to slide off the road.

And falling. Oh, God, it'd been the scariest thing I've ever experienced. Hurtling through the dark night, end over end, unable to see anything except the blur of tree limbs as they rushed by in the yellow glow of the headlights. Shattering glass, the crunch of metal. Sounds from that night filled my ears, and my heart leaped into my throat.

Irrational fear coursed through me as the SUV slid to a stop, and I cracked open my eyes. My father's large log cabin came into view, and I blew out a relieved breath as I shrugged off the vestiges of the daydream. My focus back on the cabin, I thought of Dad, and the pain of his death came rushing back full force, adding to my despair.

Donahue removed the keys from the ignition and turned to me. "You ready?"

I hesitated, my hand on the door handle as I threw a glance back at Bella. "What do I do with the dog?"

The sheriff grimaced. "Doesn't look like she's leaving you. May as well keep her until..." He trailed off, and another stabbing pain shot through my heart.

Tamping down the hurt, I turned my focus to Bella. "I've never had a dog. What do I do with her?"

"They're not too demanding." He smiled. "Just give her food and water and let her out when she needs to go out."

I shot him a dubious look. "What do I feed her?"

In all the time I'd stayed at Jack's, I really hadn't paid attention to what Bella had eaten or when. Jack had let her out from time to time, but everything else was kind of a blur. I felt completely unprepared for this—it was like having to care for another person, and the responsibility wasn't an entirely welcome one. I could barely take care of myself.

Donahue chuckled. "You really don't know much about dogs, do you?" There was no malice in his words, though, so I just shrugged amiably. "It's okay, I'll grab some food and get the rest of your things in the morning. Will you be okay here by yourself?"

I bit my lip and nodded. Worst case, I could call Brent. He was probably worried to death, anyway. Indecision gripped me as I thought about the accident that had driven me to Jack's house in the first place. Brent had been my friend for years. Surely he had nothing to do with recent events. Unless... He stood to gain a lot if I wasn't around anymore.

Unbidden, Jack's face flashed in my mind, and my heart broke all over again. I needed someone with me here tonight. Turning to Donahue, I wiped a tear from my cheek. "Can you please call Brent?"

"Of course." He hesitated, then gave a single concise nod. "Let's get you settled, and I'll take care of it."

I climbed from the car and wrapped my arms around

my waist, bracing against the cold as I made my way to the porch. The chill bit into my bones, and I cursed myself for stomping out of Jack's without even a coat.

Sheriff Donahue made quick work of letting Bella out and took the steps up to the porch in a single stride. He paused as he fished for a key. "It's been locked up for the past few days, so everything should be good, but I'm going to take a look around, just in case."

I tossed him a grateful glance. "I appreciate it."

While he checked the cabin, I headed toward the fireplace, Bella following my every move. It was cold inside from being uninhabited this past week, and I absently petted her before turning my attention to stacking the logs in the grate. To say I wasn't experienced at outdoorsy things was an understatement, and it took me several minutes to finally get the fire to light. A surge of pleasure warmed me as the tiny flame sparked to life, and I watched it grow for a moment, licking over the kindling, before pushing to my feet.

Bella still at my heels, I slunk over to the couch and sank onto the soft cushions. The dog flopped down on the floor at my feet and curled into a ball, ready for a doggy nap. I didn't blame her—it was only midafternoon and I already felt exhausted enough to sleep for the next two days. I closed my eyes and tipped my head back, turning my face to the ceiling. The back of my head still throbbed, stress from the day pounding away at my brain. I wanted to remember everything *right this minute*, but my body obviously had different ideas.

Footsteps sounded beside me, and I glanced up at the sheriff. I started to stand, but he waved me back down.

"Can I get you anything?" He dropped to a crouch

beside the couch and stretched out one hand to stroke Bella's head.

The dog shifted to her back, begging for a belly rub, and a tiny smile touched my mouth as he obliged. For a long moment, I watched the two of them, wondering what my life had come to. I had a dog, for Christ's sake. And I hated dogs. How had everything become so messed up in just the span of a few days?

I sighed and pulled my feet up, hugging a pillow to my chest. "I honestly don't know. Most of my stuff is gone, I think. Except what Jack bought me. I imagine whoever broke in took my purse and everything inside. Unless you found something?" I tacked on the last part as a question, hope infusing my voice, but he shook his head.

"Sorry. We didn't see anything."

"Of course not," I remarked bitterly. "I don't have money, a license, a phone, anything."

His chin dipped once. "I can take care of the phone. I'll get one to you this afternoon, tomorrow morning at the latest. There's a bank in town, so you should be able to transfer funds if you plan to stay for a bit. As for the license" —he spread his hands wide—"I can't do much about that. You'll just have to replace it when you get home."

I nodded miserably. "Thank you, sheriff. For everything."

A tiny smile lifted his mouth. "I think after everything that's happened, you can call me Eric." I opened my mouth to protest, but he held up a hand. "As a friend. Everyone else does."

I nodded haltingly, still not completely comfortable with the idea. "Okay."

He speared me with a gaze. "I know it's been a rough morning for you, but..." I should've known I wouldn't get out of this easily. He continued, "Can you tell me what you remember?"

I let out a soft sigh. "Some of my memory is still spotty, but I'll try to fill in the gaps."

Reluctantly, I launched into my story, telling him of the break-in and the person chasing me down the mountain. "I remember falling," I recalled, closing my eyes. That was a feeling I'd never forget. "The next thing I remember is seeing Jack, then everything went black."

"Any idea who it may have been?"

I shook my head. "No. I didn't get a good look at him."

"Brent says you had a run-in with a local man at the bar last week. Toby Brown."

"I did, but..." God, that felt so long ago. "It wasn't him. The build didn't fit."

While Toby was tall and broad, he also carried a paunch around his middle. Whoever had broken into my cabin had been significantly leaner, even under the thick fabric of the winter coat he'd been wearing.

"What about your family?"

"I'm not sure. You know about my dad's will?" Eric nodded solemnly, and I sucked in a breath. "Janine wasn't happy about it—at all. Only Brent was here with me, but..." I still didn't want to consider his involvement.

The sheriff seemed to know exactly what I was thinking because he gave a concise nod. "We're checking every avenue, but if you think of anything else, let me know." I offered a wan smile in response and he placed his hands on his thighs as if to stand, then paused. "I gave Mr. McCann a call, so he should be here shortly. I..." He paused, his gaze sliding away for a moment as he rubbed the back of his neck with one hand. "I just want you to know... We questioned both your stepmother and stepbrother after your disappearance."

"Okay." The word came out on a whisper as I watched him intently, waiting on pins and needles.

"They were both cleared, but... you should be extra cautious in the meantime."

I read between the lines. Although he'd questioned Brent and Janine, they were the only ones who stood to gain anything. Even though they hadn't been found guilty of anything, he hadn't completely dismissed them, either. I nodded my understanding. "Thank you for everything."

"Of course." He pushed to his feet. "Is there anything else I can do for you?"

I glanced around the room, my gaze lingering on the photographs gracing the mantle, and my heart clenched. "Any chance you can dig up a couple boxes for me?"

"Can do." He glanced around the cabin before meeting my eyes again. "Will you be leaving, or...?"

He let the words trail off, and I had to look away from his penetrating stare. I really had no idea what the hell I was going to do. Maybe it was better for everyone involved if I just left. Screw the business. Now that I knew Jack was Dad's partner—my new partner—I didn't really want anything to do with Hamilton Construction. Not right now, anyway. He'd surely do a better job than I would. I wondered if there was any way that I could find a loophole in Dad's will. Maybe I could just pawn the damn thing off on Jack and wash my hands of it—and him.

I shook my head. "I haven't decided. I just can't look at all this stuff right now."

"I understand." He hesitated, looking like he wanted to say something else. I tipped my head in question, and he rubbed his forehead. "Look. I know it's not my place, but... Just think about what I said in the car, would you?"

A conciliatory smile lifted the corners of my mouth. "I'll try."

A commotion outside drew our attention to the front door, and Bella leapt to her feet, wary of the newcomer. Brent swept inside, his eyes wide and frantic until they landed on me. The relief in his expression was palpable. "Oh, my God! Amelia, I was so worried about you!"

Bella let out a ferocious growl, her entire body quivering as she placed herself in front of me. I patted the dog on the head and ordered her to lie down. She hesitated for a moment, glancing between Brent and me before resuming her spot on the floor.

Donahue and I shared a quick look as I stood and turned my attention back to Brent. "Come in."

He inspected the German shepherd with obvious surprise before dismissing her and crossing the room, sliding to a stop in front of the couch and pulling me into his arms. Despite the look of relief on his face, I automatically stiffened at the show of affection, my body tensing with anxiety. I stood rigid in his embrace, enduring the hug until he finally loosened his hold. He pulled back and gazed down at me, hands still resting on my upper arms as he inspected me. "You okay?"

I smiled and shrugged him off, ignoring the look of hurt that crossed his face. "I'm fine, Brent. Really."

"What happened?" He threw an angry look at the sheriff. "They wouldn't tell us anything."

"Don't blame Sheriff Donahue," I admonished. "He didn't know anything until today either."

At Brent's confused look, I gestured to the couch with a resigned sigh. "You'd better sit. It's a long story."

TWO

Mia

Bella and Sheriff Donahue watched Brent with identical expressions of cautious curiosity, and I had to fight to bite back a smile. The sheriff met my eyes and raised his brows, a silent question to make sure everything was okay. I gave a slight nod, and he excused himself with the promise once more to get me a phone and my things as well as Bella's.

Brent sank down on the couch as the front door slammed behind the sheriff, and I stood there, studying my stepbrother. He'd once been my only true friend; now I had no idea if I could trust him or not.

For nearly a full minute, we stared at each other, unsure of what to say. His voice was quiet, his demeanor subdued when he finally spoke. "What happened?"

I needed to find out if he had anything to do with my accident, but I wasn't sure I wanted to delve into that just yet. More than anything, I just needed someone familiar; I wanted an ear to listen and a shoulder to cry on.

"I was in a car accident." Brent sucked in a sharp

breath, and I studied his expression, debating how much to tell him. "I managed to get to a house and the man took care of me. Sheriff Donahue picked me up today and brought me back."

Although I'd been angry and in a hurry, I should have packed everything while I was there. I hadn't allowed myself to dwell on it before, but now the question rose up in front of me—had I left my things behind as an excuse to see him again?

My heart cracked a little more, and I shoved the pain down. If I was going to pour my heart out, I was going to need some coffee. I couldn't seem to get warm, couldn't push down the darkness that threatened to swallow me whole.

"But..." His brows drew together in confusion as he watched me. "I don't understand. Why didn't you tell me you were going somewhere? I thought..." He trailed off, his eyes widening as if something had suddenly occurred to him. "Were you leaving?"

Averting my eyes, I pinned them to the wall just over his shoulder. He looked so earnest, so sincere. I forced my gaze back to his. "I'm going to make a cup of coffee, then I'll tell you everything. Do you want some?"

He nodded, silently studying me. The mundane task of making coffee was a welcome distraction, but it was over all too soon, and I sank onto the couch and passed Brent a mug. With a deep breath, I launched into the events leading up to the accident and subsequent rescue—all the parts I could remember.

He looked stricken at the news, like he had no idea what had forced me from the cabin in the first place. "And this man... he took care of you?"

I refused to look at him, but I could hear the obvious

curiosity in his tone. Brent no doubt thought the worst, that I'd been held against my will, potentially threatened or raped. He let out a relieved sigh when I nodded. "We should thank him. Maybe we can send him something."

I shook my head and set my mug on the coffee table. "I don't think that's a good idea. It's... He..."

"Did he hurt you?" Brent's brows furrowed in concern, his tone dropping to a threatening growl, and I rushed to reassure him.

"No. He didn't hurt me." Not physically, anyway. Though the scratches and contusions covering my body had begun to fade, my heart was now battered and bruised. I twisted my hands together nervously in my lap as I tried to form the words. "But there's something else. The man who rescued me? It was..."

I paused, unable to continue, and Brent stared at me expectantly. "Is it someone we know?" I nodded. "Well?" he prompted. "Who is it?"

I bit my lip and finally met his gaze. "Jack."

"Jack?" He did a double take. "*Jack?*"

I smiled sadly. His reaction would have been amusing, but the situation was too serious and I was much too fragile. If I started to laugh, I was afraid I'd break down and sob until I had no tears left to shed.

He stared at me, astounded, opening and closing his mouth several times as if unable to form words. "Like... your Jack?"

My Jack... A lump formed in my throat, and I swallowed it down as I nodded once more.

He shook his head in disbelief. "Jesus. Who would've thought?"

I let out a bitter laugh. "Trust me, he was the last person I expected to see."

"But..." His brow drew together. "He never said anything. Why?"

I lifted a shoulder. "He said he didn't know who to trust."

He turned a pair of concerned eyes on me as the severity of the situation sank in. "Are you okay? Do you want to talk about it?"

I studied my stepbrother. Although my memory was still spotty, he was familiar. He'd been my friend for the past few years, and he'd always been there when I needed him. I didn't know if I could fully trust him, but he knew me better than most people, and he was aware of my past with Jack. I needed to talk with someone and get these riotous emotions off my chest.

When I remained silent, he continued, undaunted. "Amelia—"

"Mia," I automatically corrected. After a beat of silence, I glanced up to meet his gaze. Belatedly I realized what I'd said. Brent stared at me, and I immediately tried to backpedal. "You know, I mean..." I dropped my gaze to where my hands lay in my lap, tears stinging my eyelids.

Jack had been the only one to call me Mia. After our divorce, I'd shunned the nickname, insisting instead on going by my full name. After only a handful of days, Jack had twisted me up, made me question everything. It was like the past eight years had never even existed, as if Jack and I had picked up right where we'd left off. He'd changed me over the past few days, in more ways than one—and I would never be the same.

I watched through blurry, teary eyes as Brent set his mug on the coffee table and scooted closer. A second later I felt his hand on my shoulder. "I'm sorry."

I had no idea what he was apologizing for. Maybe for

bringing up bad memories or arguing with me. Whatever the reason, my battered heart and bruised emotions appreciated the gesture. "It's okay."

He sighed and dropped his hand away. "It's not. Mia," he started, then stopped. Taking a deep breath, he plunged forward. "I didn't say anything before, but... do you think maybe this happened for a reason?"

I lifted my head and met his inquisitive gaze. "What do you mean?"

He focused on a point over my shoulder before finally meeting my eyes again. "Of all the people in the world you could have ended up with, it was Jack."

Goosebumps raced up my arms, but I didn't have a chance to speak as he continued.

"You can call that coincidence, but... don't you think it's a little odd? I mean, after everything that's happened?"

Were I not so furious with the entire situation, I might be able to concede his point. Part of me wanted to—a huge part of me. My heart wanted it to be true more than anything. Had fate dropped me into Jack's life for a reason? The connection between us was undeniable. Was it truly mere coincidence that I'd ended up at his place? Or had some divine intervention guided me and helped me to find him again?

Mere weeks ago I'd wondered where he was and what he was doing. Now I knew. He and my father had stayed in touch and were probably closer than ever, considering they were business partners—and I was still the odd one out.

Old insecurities flared up, and stubborn pride kicked in. "There's no such thing as coincidence. Besides," I scoffed, "I wouldn't have even been on this godforsaken mountain had my father not orchestrated this whole ridiculous thing."

His lips flattened into a thin line, his expression

completely unconvinced by my staunch refusal. "You must be right."

His dubiousness irritated me, and I scooped up the coffee mug just to give my hands something to do. "Of course I am."

He gave a clipped nod, then finally, blessedly, dropped the subject. "What are your plans for tomorrow?"

I gazed around the cabin, my hands tightening around the mug. This was one reason I'd come all the way up here initially. I needed to put Dad's things to rights. My heart tightened at the prospect. "I think I'll go through some of Dad's old stuff."

Brent shot me a concerned look. "Do you want some company?"

"No, thanks." I shook my head. "I think this is something I need to do alone."

"All right."

Silence descended as I stared at the pictures on the mantle. Some memories were clear as day, but other pieces of my past remained elusively out of reach.

Why would I spend one more second with you?

Cold washed over me as I conjured the memory. No matter how hard I tried, I couldn't get those words out of my head. And yet... How many times had he told me this past week how much he cared for me? He'd spewed words of love and regret. How much could he have possibly loved me if he just threw me away, like I'd meant nothing to him? He clearly regretted the past—or, at least, he acted like he did— but anyone could apologize for their actions without meaning it.

That snippet of conversation was so clear, the words damning, but a niggle of unease slithered down my spine. Despite everything I'd learned, I couldn't help but feel that something wasn't quite right. Jack said he'd screwed up. What had he meant by that? Did he regret walking away, or was there more to the story? I'd only remembered bits of pieces so far, but I couldn't remember what had precipitated the conversation.

I turned to my stepbrother, who knew me better than anyone. "Hey, Brent?"

His brows lifted in silent question, and I dropped my gaze away, toying with the fabric of the throw draped over the arm of the couch. "When Jack and I split up... did I ever tell you the whole story?"

He remained quiet, and I peered up at him. Finally, he shrugged. "You didn't want to talk about it, so I never asked. All I knew was that he hurt you."

As if that made all the difference in the world. I'd been heartbroken, so Brent had automatically chosen to support me. "Okay."

"Is that all?"

Was it? I had no idea. The past few days had been so real, but I felt like a piece of the puzzle still didn't quite fit. "Yeah. I think so."

"All right." He stood, and I did the same, following him as he made his way to the front door. "I guess I'll talk to you later, then."

After a beat, he moved closer and pulled me into a one-armed hug, briskly running one hand over my upper arm affectionately. "Just remember, I'm right down the road if you need me."

"I know." I smiled at him, but if anything, his expression became even more intense.

"I know you don't ask for help very often, Mia. But everyone needs help sometimes."

My throat constricted with tears, and I dropped my

gaze to the polished oak floors. Swallowing hard, I pushed the words out. "I know."

Without another word, he kissed my temple and strode toward the door. I glanced up just as his hand landed on the knob. "Hey."

He looked over his shoulder at me, his face expectant.

"Thank you."

"You're welcome." Brent smiled and pulled open the door, disappearing into the cold darkness.

I stood in the doorway, watching the taillights disappear in the swirling snow, allowing the frigid air to nip at my skin. If only for a moment, the numbness began to recede, dulling the sting of hurt and betrayal. Closing the door, I locked up and leaned against the cool wood, tipping my head to the ceiling and closing my eyes.

Now that Brent was gone, I was filled with a strange combination of relief and disappointment. I still wasn't sure exactly what to think. Did he have anything to do with the break-in or not? I couldn't tell. His expression and his attitude had been sincere enough. But what if something simmered below the surface? Something that I couldn't see?

With a sigh, I pushed off the door and made my way up to the bedroom. Toenails clicked against the hardwood floors as Bella jumped up from her spot and fell into step behind me. The lights still blazed on the first floor, but they lent a sense of security. I couldn't bear to sit here alone in the dark, wondering at every creak and groan. And likely it wouldn't matter anyway. I doubted I'd get a wink of sleep.

Emotionally exhausted, I crawled into the bed and pulled the covers up to my chin. Seconds later, I felt Bella hop up and settle at the foot of the bed. Just having her here made me feel immeasurably better. I knew no one would get past her. Not even Jack. Even though he was her master, she hadn't hesitated to place herself between me and him this afternoon to protect me from harm.

Inevitably, my thoughts turned back to him. Jack had been wrong to mislead me. He'd been wrong to lie, though I understood why he'd done it. Worse than that though, there was one thing I couldn't deny no matter how hard I tried: I still loved him. I always would.

THREE

Jack

I had no idea how long I stood there, a myriad of emotions rendering me motionless. Like a crack in glass, I felt the fracture splinter into a spiderweb of fissures, radiating slowly from my heart outward to my fingertips. Finally, my legs buckled under the heavy shroud of pain, and I crumpled to the floor. Head in my hands, I allowed the pain to overtake me.

I'd known this would happen—I deserved it. I'd hoped to hell she would understand, that I could make her see, but our time had run out. She'd recovered her memory and the new, wonderful memories we'd made over the past week apparently weren't enough to overcome eight years' worth of pain and unrest.

I sat there, watching the shadows lengthen against the wall, as if Mia's departure had sucked the light and love from the cabin. When I could no longer stand it, I pushed to my feet and used the bathroom, then trudged to the couch. I didn't dare venture toward the bedroom, even as the sky turned black with night. I couldn't bear to see the bed where we'd made love, where we'd poured our hearts out and promised to love each other forever.

It'd all been a lie—and I had no one to blame but myself. Slumping down into the corner of the couch, I stared at the empty fireplace. The cabin was cold but I couldn't muster the energy to care. My heart was already frozen, as numb as my ass from sitting on the cold, hard floor. It was as if the life had drained from my body, leaving nothing but an empty void.

Tipping my head back, I gazed sightlessly at the ceiling. Memories assaulted me; I remembered the first time we'd met, the electric feeling that had coursed through my body. It was the same thing I still felt every time I looked at her. Now I felt nothing.

I dozed fitfully, awakened constantly by the recurring nightmare of watching her walk away. Finally, just after dawn I stumbled to the kitchen. Forgoing the coffeepot, I pulled a tumbler from the cabinet and grabbed a bottle of whiskey from the shelf. Settling into an oak chair, I stared over the table at the empty seat across from me. *Her chair.* She should be sitting here with me now, talking and laughing. We'd share breakfast, then I'd carry her back to the bedroom where we would make love again.

Except it would never happen. She would never fill that space again—not at this table and not in my life. I'd told myself in the beginning that it would never work out, but no amount of consideration could have ever prepared me for the reality of having to watch her walk away. It had damn near killed me the first time. How could I let her go again?

For years, I'd silently watched over her as she'd grown from a restless young girl into a strong, independent, beautiful woman. Despite her memory loss, there was a surety to her, a silent confidence that hadn't been there all those years ago. These last few days had reminded me of just how good we were together, almost as if nothing had changed. Although, that wasn't quite true—it was better. I'd fallen even deeper and harder than I could have imagined. I loved her with all my heart, and I chose to do the one thing that would make her happiest: let her go.

I twisted the glass in my hands. With any luck, the alcohol would dim the pain, the effects seeping into my skin, then deeper into my bones until my body began to shut down and it finally took my misery away.

I closed my eyes and sipped the lukewarm whiskey, my mouth twisting in a grimace at the temperature. It needed ice, but I was too damn lazy to get up and get it. Besides, all I cared about at the moment was getting drunk. I didn't give a damn how I got that way, as long as it would allow me to forget. Draining the remainder of the glass, I wiped my mouth with the back of my hand and poured another shot. Then another. And another.

Through my muddled thoughts, I heard a banging on the front door. Not bothering to tear my eyes from the tumbler in front of me, I poured another shot, watching the amber liquid slosh against the sides of the glass.

The banging continued, and Donahue's voice filtered through the thick wood. "Prescott! Open the fuck up!"

I took another swig, hoping Tennessee's finest would start to kick in soon. I could still feel the pain, just as fresh and excruciating as the moment she'd walked out of my life —again.

The banging stopped, and the door opened, then slammed closed again behind Donahue. I barely glanced up as the sheriff came to a stop beside me, his expression one of intense annoyance—and relief.

"You expect a crime scene?"

"Wasn't sure what the hell to expect, to be honest," Eric snapped. "Thanks for letting me pound on the door for ten minutes, asshole."

I returned my gaze to the whiskey. "It was two minutes."

"What the hell ever. And goddamn, it's cold as fuck in here. Trying to freeze to death?"

The sarcasm in Eric's tone died away when I remained silent. Propping his hands on his hips, the sheriff studied me for several seconds. I was acutely aware of his intense gaze, yet I couldn't bring myself to look at him. I refused to acknowledge the pity that would surely be written all over his face.

Despite Eric's concern, I wasn't selfish or cowardly enough to take my own life. It was almost a shame that I was too damn stubborn to give in to the pain threatening to pull me under. It wasn't death I feared, not really. The pathetic reality was that I didn't want to live without Mia. It was an impossible situation. Endure the torment of seeing her move on with life—again—knowing I could never be part of it, or end my life and never have the chance to see her again. No, I couldn't risk that. I'd rather spend an eternity watching her from afar than never see her beautiful face again.

With a soft exhalation, Eric moved away from the table, and some of the tension fled from my muscles, momentarily free of the other man's scrutiny. I heard him moving around the living room, and the sound of logs being stacked in the grate followed by the catch of kindling reached my ears. The footsteps came closer again, and the sheriff sank into the chair across from me. Mia's chair.

I opened my mouth, ready to snap at the man. Just as quickly, I closed it. Didn't matter anyway, since she was never coming back. My eyes flicked upward, colliding with Eric's penetrating green-brown gaze. I steeled myself under his level stare, and I finally caved with a sigh of resignation.

"If you're gonna sit here, at least have a fucking drink."

Eric shook his head. "I'm on duty."

"Then get the hell out."

Eric glared at me for a good ten seconds. "You at least gonna get your lazy ass up to get me a glass?"

I arched a brow, and his lips thinned. Heaving his big body out of the chair, he threw a caustic look over his shoulder. "You're kind of a dick, you know that?"

I bobbed my head. "Seems to be the general consensus."

Eric's stride faltered momentarily before carrying him across the kitchen. Throwing open cabinet doors until he finally found what he was looking for, he pulled down a glass and stomped back to the table. He snagged the bottle of whiskey and sloshed two fingers into the tumbler, then set the bottle off to the side, out of my reach.

Twisting my now empty glass in one hand, I glanced between Eric and the whiskey. "Plan on finishin' that off?"

He snorted. "As long as you don't. Do I even want to know how much you've had?"

"Not nearly enough," I snapped. I shoved the glass away and crossed my arms over my chest, itching for a fight, daring him to antagonize me.

I could only imagine the image I painted. Still in yesterday's clothes, half drunk, with two days of stubble, even I hated me right now. No fucking wonder Mia had left. Hell, even the damn dog had followed her out the door. That had probably hurt the worst. Bella had looked at me with those huge soulful eyes, as if assessing me and finding me responsible for Mia's unhappiness. She'd determined that Mia needed her more than I did, and my heart ached. I'd driven literally everyone away.

"You holding up?"

I rolled my eyes. So, I hadn't driven *everyone* away. "For a smart man, you ask some stupid fucking questions."

The corners of his lips twitched. "Part of the job description."

We descended into silence again, and I wondered what Mia was doing at this very moment. Was she with Brent, enjoying her time at the resort? Was she safe? Despite everything, I couldn't—wouldn't—let anything happen to her. I'd crawl on my hands and knees, grovel, beg, and plead. I'd literally do anything to get her to look at me the way she once had. Too bad she didn't seem inclined to give me the time of day, let alone a chance to explain myself.

Although, really, I didn't have much of an excuse. I'd been greedy for time with her, no matter the cost. And I'd paid the price—dearly. The look she'd sent me as she walked out the door still had the power to bring me to my knees. In those baby blues had lain disappointment, anger, and a devastation so intense it cut me like a knife.

"You look like shit."

I rolled my eyes. "Thanks, asshole."

"If it's any consolation," he murmured, "she looked almost as bad as you when I dropped her off."

My heart clenched and my stomach roiled. It wasn't a consolation—not at all. I never wanted Mia to feel pain, especially not pain that I'd caused. She deserved nothing but happiness and joy. Now she was miserable. Because of me. I gripped the glass so hard I was surprised it didn't shatter.

Eric opened his mouth, closed it again. He fidgeted with

his glass, sliding it back and forth across the smooth oak table.

Each movement raised my ire. "You may as well cut to the chase and say whatever the fuck you're thinking."

A myriad of emotions flitted across the other man's face, and he took a sip of whiskey. Irritated and on edge, I was almost at my breaking point when he finally spoke. "I don't know exactly what happened here," he began slowly, "but I believe you had her best interests at heart."

I swallowed hard, my gaze dropping back to the glass clenched in my hands. Finally, I nodded. "I always have. She doesn't see it that way, though," I said softly.

Eric canted his head to one side. "I don't know about that." At my wry glance, the sheriff chuckled. "Oh, she was seven shades of pissed, don't get me wrong."

My chin dropped to my chest at the admission, all trace of hope evaporating, my heart plummeting to my toes.

"But," he continued, "she's a smart girl. I think once she calms down, she'll see the situation for what it really was."

I hummed noncommittally, not believing a word.

"It's a lot to absorb," he insisted. "Give her some time to sort out what happened, how she's feeling. She'll be back."

God, how I wanted to believe that. But I knew better. She'd walked away once before—she wouldn't hesitate to do it again. She believed she deserved better than me, and I'd just proved it to her. Again.

"No." The word broke as it left my lips. "She won't."

"She will."

"She wouldn't spit on me if I were on fire."

A brief smile flashed across Eric's face before it slipped away. We remained silent for a long minute, the only sound the faint clink of the glass against the wood.

"I see a lot of people in my line of work, you know."

The comment came from left field, and I lifted a brow at him, not entirely sure where this conversation was headed. "And? What the hell does that mean?"

"Just sayin', I've met my fair share of people in bad situations."

I swallowed hard, thoughts of Mia threatening to consume me. I'd put her in an impossible situation and expected her to deal with it. It hadn't been fair to her, not at all.

His voice cut through my musings. "Listen, man. Over the years, I've gotten pretty good at reading people. Trust me when I say she's hurting and angry—but she doesn't hate you."

I scoffed and tensed as he leaned forward in his chair.

"You don't look the way she did if you hate someone. That woman"—he jabbed a finger eastward, toward the lodge—"loves you. It was written all over her face. Give her a little bit of time and space to process what happened."

I wiped a shaky hand down my face. "It's not that easy."

"Then you don't want her badly enough."

I slammed the glass down and leaned forward in my chair. "I'd do anything for her! Don't fucking sit there and tell me it's not enough."

Rage had my entire body quaking, my blood pulsing through my veins. Hazel eyes stared unblinking at me, and I glared back.

Finally, Eric nodded. "I believe you. Now you just have to convince her."

I dropped my head into my hands. How could I make her see? I'd done everything wrong; I'd hurt her so badly. Not once—but twice. I didn't deserve another chance.

I shook my head as I rose from the chair. "Just do me a favor and keep her safe."

"Jack." My name falling from the other man's lips was a warning, a plea to listen.

Silently, I plodded to the sink and set my glass inside, staring out the window at the vast landscape, cold and barren—exactly the way I felt. I turned to him. "There has to be a connection. Find it. And don't let anything happen to her."

His eyes narrowed. "You know—"

I pushed off the counter and headed toward my office. "Bella's food and bowls are in the pantry. Lock up behind you."

A litany of cuss words followed me, but I stared blindly ahead until I entered my sanctuary and locked the door behind me. Emotions bubbled to the surface, but I refused to acknowledge them. I needed to push everything down and lock it up tight where it couldn't hurt me. And the best way I knew to deal with that was work. Slumping into the soft leather chair, I powered on my laptop.

Pulling up the spreadsheets, I began to sift through the shell corporations one by one. Everything had been quiet for the past week or so, and I wondered if Mia's arrival—and subsequent disappearance—had thrown a wrench in someone's plans. Eventually the embezzler would slip up, and I planned to catch him in the act. God as my witness, if the person responsible had hurt Mia... My blood boiled. There would be hell to pay.

FOUR

Mia

I lay in bed, staring vacantly at the ceiling. I had no idea how long I'd been looking at the same spot, a little knot in the pine that looked vaguely like a splintered heart. Or maybe I was just seeing what I wanted to see. My eyes had been drawn to it, like the tiny mark was a reflection of the pain that seared my soul. I felt shredded inside, torn to ribbons, as though the pieces might never fit together again. The only thing that had made me feel whole, complete, was Jack. But he'd lied to me, taken my trust and smashed it into a thousand pieces, heedless of the ramifications.

My eyes felt swollen and tender, and it felt like gritty sandpaper rubbing against my eyelids every time I blinked. Another tear slid free, coasting down my cheek and slipping onto the pillow. How many tears had soaked the fabric over the course of the past eight hours? Hundreds? Thousands, maybe? I was surprised I had any tears left to shed.

My heart had broken all over again as I'd poured every ounce of agony from my body. I didn't want to think, didn't want to move. All I wanted was to close my eyes, curl up into a little ball, and forget that the past few days had happened.

Except... I didn't. Despite everything that had happened, I didn't want to take back a second of my time spent with Jack. He'd lied to me, yes. But he'd made me laugh. Made me love. For the first time in almost a decade, I'd been truly happy. But now it was over.

I squeezed my eyes closed as another tear seeped out. God, would I ever forget the feel of his hands on me, the way he'd touched my body, my heart and soul? I curled onto my side and drew my knees to my chest, grief contorting my body into a tiny ball. Bella lifted her head from where she lay next to me and nudged my hand. With a watery smile, I ran my fingers through the dog's thick fur, petting her head and down her sleek back. Not once since I'd returned here had the dog abandoned me, and for that I was grateful. It lessened the sting, though not by much. Almost against my will, I'd come to care for the dog a great deal. It would tear me apart to have to let her go when I left.

I still felt cold all over, as if ice streamed through my veins. Even Bella's snuggles couldn't make up for what I was missing. I appreciated the dog's effort to comfort me, but it wasn't enough. I missed Jack's familiar weight at my back, his heavy arm settled securely over me. I missed him. Desperately. Wholly. With every molecule of my body. I felt like a shell of my former self. Like a porcelain vase that had been glued back together after being broken, I felt every fracture, every crevice, as if the pieces didn't quite fit. And without Jack, I might never be whole again.

Refusing to dwell on thoughts of the past or what the future might bring, I threw the covers aside. I'd tossed and turned all night and hadn't slept a wink. Every time I closed my eyes, I was assaulted by another memory. Snippets of the past flashed brightly in front of my eyes, dragging me deeper into the dark abyss of dreary, dismal pain.

Every inch of my body hurt, from the top of my head to the tips of my toes, aching from the bone-deep agony of loss. I forced my feet to move and haltingly made my way to the bathroom. A hot shower revived my fatigued muscles, but my heart still felt bruised.

I headed downstairs and made a beeline for the fridge. My crying jag had left me practically dehydrated, and I pulled out a bottle of water and gulped it down. My stomach still felt twisted in knots, and I knew that eating anything was out of the question.

I'd just started the coffeepot when Bella's ears perked up and she let out a low woof. The muffled sound of tires on the snow-covered gravel drive caught my attention seconds later, and I drifted toward the front door. I peeked out the sidelight and watched as an SUV bearing the Sheriff's Office logo slid to a stop near the front porch. Eric Donahue climbed from the driver seat, then rounded the back of the vehicle and retrieved a handful of bags. I opened the door and held it wide as he entered the house.

Bella danced around his legs, and I gently admonished her. "Bella! Go lie down."

The dog threw me a look before slinking over to her spot in front of the couch and collapsing with a sigh. Eric and I exchanged a grin as I closed the door and extricated the shopping bags from his hands. "Thanks."

I watched, bemused, as he shifted the huge bag of dog food from his shoulder and dropped it to the floor with a thud. He shrugged and smiled. "I wasn't sure how long you planned to keep her, so..."

My smile turned brittle at the offhand remark, and I

could feel the sheriff's eyes on me as I turned on a heel and carried the bags to the kitchen, dumping them unceremoniously in the center of the table. His hawklike gaze trailed me as I strode to the counter and picked up my coffee, then moved to the living room and dropped to the couch.

Eric moved efficiently around the cabin, saying nothing as he dumped the water from the porcelain bowl I'd filled for her last night, then placed it in the sink to be washed. Setting her matching silver bowls on the floor, he dumped dog food into one and filled the other with water. Bella jumped to her feet, her tail beating the air as she happily trotted over at the prospect of food.

Guilt slammed into me. I should be helping, not wallowing in my own pity. "I'm sorry."

Eric waved me off. "No worries." He paused and tipped his chin toward the mug in my hand. "I'll take a cup of coffee, though, if you have some."

"Of course. Help yourself."

He chuckled. "Seems to be a common theme today."

I canted my head at the strange remark, but the sheriff didn't elaborate. He moved around the kitchen, doctoring his coffee before leaning against the counter. Sipping his brew, he studied me. "You doing okay?"

I lifted one shoulder and directed my gaze at the stone fireplace. "Fine, I guess." The sheriff was still a stranger to me and yet... he was a friend. He'd gone out of his way for me. "Thank you. For everything."

"No problem." He shrugged. "We've been slow, so it's no big deal. Plus the coffee is better here."

I smiled at his teasing tone, but it just as quickly slipped from my face. "I assume you stopped by Jack's place this morning?"

"I did."

"How is..." I lifted a hand, then curled it into a fist and dropped it to my lap. "Is he...?"

Donahue offered me a soft smile. "As well as can be expected."

I was still mad at him—furious, in fact. But it upset me to know that he was hurting too. Deep down I knew he'd done what he thought was right.

Finally he cleared his throat. "I contacted a rental agency that will drop off a car for you. Hopefully they'll get it over here this afternoon." His handsome features twisted into an apologetic smile. "I'd have asked what kind of car you preferred, but they don't have much of a selection."

"It's fine." I waved away his concern. Just the thought of driving again was enough to send shivers down my spine. In all my life, I didn't think I'd ever forget the feeling of dropping hundreds of feet through the air and slamming into the earth.

Donahue must have seen the involuntary shudder wrack my body, because he moved closer and settled into the chair to my right. "You okay?" I nodded and he continued. "You been feeling okay? No blackouts, no dizziness?"

Inquisitive eyes met mine, and I knew what he was asking. There was no way he'd let me drive if I wasn't up to it. "I haven't had any issues—other than the memory loss."

"I know you've been toughing it out, but there's a hospital down in Kalispell."

I shook my head. "I'll be fine. Really," I emphasized when he lifted a brow. "I feel okay physically. It's just... I think it was too much for my mind to process."

He nodded. "I understand. And I just want you to know that we're checking every possible lead. If there's anything you can think of, anything you remember..."

Desperation was evident in his tone, and I wished I

could help. At this point, there was nothing new, just the same memories looping through my mind over and over. "I'm sorry." I shrugged helplessly.

"It's okay." He offered a soft smile.

Silence stretched between us for several minutes as we sipped our coffee. I could tell he wanted to say something, ask me a hundred questions, but he didn't. Eric's body was tense and coiled, as if ready to move at any second, so much like Jack, and I almost smiled at the comparison. They were two of a kind, though they probably didn't like to admit it. I don't know when I'd started thinking of him as Eric instead of calling him by his last name or his title of sheriff. If not a friend, exactly, he'd been supportive and helpful, and I appreciated his concern.

Out of the corner of my eye, I watched his knee bounce restlessly, as if some part of him had to constantly be moving. It was on the tip of my tongue to tell him it was okay to go when, without a word, he stood and strode to the table. He scooped up a white plastic bag bearing a familiar logo, then crossed the room and extended it to me. "I picked this up for you this morning."

I accepted the bag with an appreciative smile and dug out the new phone and charger. "Thank you."

He settled back into the chair and balanced his elbows on his knees as he spoke. "If you need anything, don't hesitate to call. I don't think someone would be stupid enough to try to break in twice, but you never know. I checked the locks when I was here last time, and everything seemed to be okay. Still, just keep an eye out for anything strange."

His words triggered another memory. "Do you know how they got in the first time?"

I assumed they'd come in through the front, but now I began to wonder. I vaguely remembered the door still being locked as I'd made my escape, so they'd either locked it behind them or come in somewhere else.

"We found footprints leading around the side of the cabin to the back door. I'm guessing they came in through the laundry room." Donahue rubbed the back of his neck. "What's interesting is there was no damage to the knob or to the door itself. So it was either unlocked, or..."

It took only a second for me to read between the lines. Someone had a way of getting in—someone had a key.

Holy shit.

I didn't know what to do with that piece of information. Somehow, that made the situation more dire, more real. If the intruder had a key, it was obviously someone close to my father. The only person I could think of that he'd trust with a key was Jack. And I knew without a doubt it hadn't been him. He'd been far too surprised at my arrival. So, if not him, then who?

I turned expectant eyes on Sheriff Donahue. "Any of your leads pan out?"

He shook his head, his tone wary as if he were cautiously choosing his words. "We don't have anything substantial yet."

I wasn't an idiot. I knew they still suspected Brent. What the hell was I going to do if it was him? My heart felt like it was breaking in my chest. Everything was spiraling out of control, falling apart more quickly than I could put it back together.

Bella trotted toward us, evidently finished with her morning meal, and flopped to the floor at my feet. I petted her head, the dog's presence reminding me that I wasn't alone.

He studied her for a minute before turning to me. "You sure you're good?"

A tight smile lifted my mouth, but I knew it didn't reach my eyes. "I'll be okay. I'm just going to stick around here today, take care of some things."

His gaze flitted around the cabin before he nodded. "Let me grab those boxes for you."

I followed him, waiting in the foyer as he carried them inside and set them by the table.

"I appreciate it." I waved a hand. "All of this. Thank you."

"No problem at all." He moved toward the front door with a tip of his chin. "I'll keep you posted."

"Okay."

"Oh, by the way," he threw over his shoulder, "I took the liberty of programming a couple important numbers in there. Just in case."

With that last cryptic remark, he was gone.

I flipped the lock and watched through the sidelight as the SUV turned out of the snow-covered driveway and disappeared through the thick green trees lining the road. Turning back around, I rested for a moment against the cool wood of the door. My gaze landed on the boxes beside the table, and my heart twisted in my chest. Steeling myself, I took a deep breath and glanced around the cabin. No time like the present. I carried my nearly empty mug to the sink and dumped it, then grabbed a box and headed upstairs.

Emotion clogged my throat as I opened the closet doors and saw the row of clothes hanging there. Mostly work clothes, flannel shirts and jeans, interspersed with the occasional dress shirt and pair of slacks. I took each article down, one by one, and neatly folded it, placing it inside the box. My fingers stroked the collar of a blue flannel shirt that I remembered well.

He'd worn it the last time I'd seen him. We'd met up for

dinner in Seattle after a photo shoot I'd done in Puget Sound. I refused to go back to Spokane, refused to acknowledge the past I'd left behind. I was cold and aloof, still furious with him. The memory brought tears to my eyes, and they slipped down my cheeks.

I couldn't bring myself to think about Jack right now. He'd lied to me, betrayed me. Yet he'd looked absolutely crushed when I'd walked out the door. Maybe the sheriff was right—there was a reason Jack had done what he did. He'd said it was for my own good and to protect me from harm. But was that the truth or what he wanted me to believe?

Why would I spend one more second with you?

Those awful words came back to me, chilling me to the bone. He'd left me behind once. What would stop him from doing it again? Could I truly trust him? Without my memory, I had no idea. Maybe once all the pieces fell into place, I could make a better decision. Until then, I would push it far from my mind—much like the clothes that I packed into the boxes.

Once the box was full, I closed it up, tucking one flap under the other to secure it. Debating where to store it for now, I glanced around the cabin. The laundry room was out of the way—I wouldn't have to trip over them or see them all the time—so I headed in that direction. I remembered what Donahue had told me about the break-in. Dropping the box to the floor, I scooted it against the door as a barrier. No way was someone getting in again without me knowing.

I spent the remainder of the afternoon packing Dad's things and cleaning the cabin from top to bottom, and it reminded me of being at Jack's house. I'd done the same thing only days ago, and it seemed that every little thing I did reminded me of my husband—my *ex-husband*.

Angrily, I dashed more tears from my cheeks. It was almost inconceivable that I could still cry after the past day and a half, yet there seemed to be a never-ending supply of tears. Mad at everyone, but mostly myself, I sank down on the couch and curled into a tiny ball, hugging a pillow to my chest. I closed my eyes against the memories assaulting me, but they came anyway. Was everyone destined to leave me?

My relationship with Dad had been strained, mostly because of my stubbornness. Was I pushing everyone away? My heart plummeted to the floor as something struck me. Maybe the problem was me. Admittedly, I'd been young and immature, running from my problems rather than facing them head-on. I wondered how Dad had felt about everything. He'd reached out to me, yes, but out of true desire to rectify things or out of obligation?

I wanted to believe that he'd truly cared about me. The photographs on the mantle bespoke as much, didn't they? And he had a book that my photos had been published in. That meant something, didn't it?

I blinked my eyes open, and a stack of magazines beneath the coffee table caught my eye. I hadn't even noticed the small shelf below the table when I'd been here previously, and I pulled the magazines into my lap. All travel magazines. I curiously flipped through the glossy pages. One page was dog-eared, and I took a closer look at the images across the spread. My breath caught as I noticed one of my own. Brows drawing together, I set the magazine aside and picked up another. I immediately flipped to the bent corner and noticed another photo I'd taken, this one in Romania.

I had no idea how long I sat there, surrounded by my own photographs. Dad had kept them all—every one. A combination of grief and guilt caused my heart to pinch.

Despite his gruff exterior, despite the rift between us, he'd still been proud of me—proud enough to buy every magazine and book I'd ever published in.

Bella barked, and the hum of an engine drew my attention to the driveway. Shushing the dog, I glanced out at the unfamiliar little red car. Seconds later, a white car with a green logo on the side turned into the drive. The sheriff's words from this morning came back to me, and understanding clicked as I opened the door and stepped out onto the porch to greet them. A young man climbed out of the car and quickly explained the policy, then passed me the paperwork to sign. With a smile of thanks, I took the keys to the rental car and headed back inside.

As I closed the door, I realized that the sky was already beginning to turn pink with the setting sun. I'd managed to stay busy most of the day, but now that dusk had fallen, anxiety settled over me once again. Checking once more to make sure the door was locked, I headed into the kitchen and dropped the keys on the counter. Glancing around, I debated what to do. I still didn't feel like eating—every little thought of the past week stole my ability to breathe, making me sick to my stomach.

Leaving the lights blazing for the second night in a row, I headed upstairs and curled up in the large bed. Bella followed moments later, settling beside me. Though it was still light out, I was exhausted from lack of sleep the night before. I rolled onto my back, and the little heart-shaped knot in the wood taunted me from its place on the ceiling.

I didn't want to stay awake any longer, replaying the moment when everything had gone so wrong. Turning back to my side, I buried my head in the pillow and willed the hurt to go away.

FIVE

Mia

I was missing something, I could feel it. Feet curled beneath me, I stared at the pile of magazines spread over the coffee table. Tears sprang to my eyes as I lifted the top magazine off the stack. I still couldn't believe Dad had kept all of them. Flipping to the dog-eared page, I found the photo I was looking for. It was the very first one I'd published for a major magazine, and it'd been a huge accomplishment. It was the cornerstone of my career, yet something nagged at me, a memory tugging at the periphery of my mind. There was a significance here, but what?

There was more to the story, and I just had to know. I'd hoped that my memory would start to come back, but so far it remained just out of reach. I'd been putting off going to my father's office at Briarleigh for the past couple days, but now it was time to address old insecurities and shortcomings and piece together a past that continued to elude me. I hoped that maybe a change of environment would trigger something in my brain and open up the vault of memories locked inside.

Slipping off the couch, I went upstairs to change. I quickly threw on a sweater and jeans, then picked up my fuzzy boots. My breath caught as I turned them over in my hands. The suede was soiled and ripped from my trek up the mountain after my accident, and my mind flashed back to that night—the break in, the intruder forcing me from the house. I hadn't spoken to the sheriff yet today, and I wondered how his investigation was coming along.

I assumed that only Brent knew I was alive and well. Jack hadn't told a soul, and despite the investigation by the Sheriff's Office, I doubted word had traveled that fast. What would everyone think when I showed up today? Would the attacker strike out at me again? A shiver snaked down my spine, and I shook it off with a deep breath. Even if I didn't feel it, I needed to put on a brave front.

I quickly tugged on the boots and jogged downstairs, then swiped the keys to the rental car off the counter. Bella sauntered over to me, and I petted her head. "I'll be back in just a bit, girl."

Pulling my coat on as I stepped outside, I locked the door behind me and trudged across the snow-covered driveway to the car. It hadn't snowed much over the past few days, but the temperature remained low enough that it wasn't melting off either. I prayed that the roads had at least been cleared.

I slid behind the wheel and cranked the engine, then kicked on the defrost function to clear the windshield. While I waited for the ice to clear, I glanced over the interior. It was strange to get back behind the wheel, and apprehension gripped me as I sat frozen in the driver seat. It was almost irrational, really. I'd been driving for fifteen years, yet the accident a couple weeks ago had rendered me almost immobile with fear.

My heart beat furiously, and my mind screamed for me to go back inside. But I couldn't—I needed answers. With a deep breath, I shifted the car into gear then headed toward the lodge, my heart jumping erratically every time I rounded a curve. Memories of that night assaulted me, and my lungs threatened to make me hyperventilate. As I crested the last hill, the top of a stone chimney speared up into the sky, and I let out a relieved sigh. I'd never been so happy to see a building in my life, and I practically wept for joy as Briarleigh came fully into view.

I parked in the side lot and took a moment to gather myself before getting out of the car. If it was an employee trying to sabotage the business, I needed to be more cautious than ever. I trusted that Sheriff Donahue would do everything in his power to find the person and bring him to justice. Until then, I would hold my head high and carry on as if nothing had happened.

Shoving the door open, I made my way into the main hall and marveled at the transformation. In just a few days, it looked more like the five-star resort it was supposed to be. The drywall that just over a week ago had been raw and unfinished was now painted a hunter green, complementing the golden hue of the logs perfectly. Dozens of recessed lights lit the space, sporadically interspersed with chandeliers that appeared to be made of deer antlers. Industrial carpet covered the floor, the contemporary swirl design a neutral brown that accented the room rather than detracted from it.

A few workers milled around, and once more Donahue's words came back to me. I studied every face as I wandered through the great room. Who could it be?

Curious eyes followed my movements as I ventured farther into the room.

Arthur Langdon's head jerked up as he noticed my arrival, and he immediately cut a path toward me. "Good Lord, Miss Amelia. What happened?"

I waved a hand airily as I affected a carefree expression. "Oh, I'm fine now. I had a little accident a week or so back when my car slid off the road."

His eyes hardened. "We didn't know what to think."

"Nothing too terrible. Got a little banged up and just needed some time to heal."

It was a piss-poor excuse, but the old man took it. "Well, I'm glad to see you're okay. We *all* are."

"Thank you, Art." A genuine smile lifted my mouth. "You have no idea how much that means to me."

With the promise to check in with him later, I headed toward the back, warily scanning my surroundings. My blood thrummed rapidly through my veins, though not from fear this time. The prospect of seeing Jack was... confusing. I was mad, yes, and not entirely ready to forgive him for withholding the truth. But I cared about him, and I couldn't deny that I wanted to see him again, even if just a brief glimpse.

Rounding the corner to the employee offices, I met a familiar gaze.

"Mia." A pleased smile lit Carter's face before wariness crept into his eyes. "How are you feeling?"

I should be mad at him, too—he'd been in on the scheme as well, but I couldn't drum up the energy to care. "I'm feeling better."

"Good, I'm glad to hear that."

My skin crawled with nervous anxiety, and I couldn't help it anymore—my eyes darted toward the oak door at the end of the hall. He followed my gaze over his shoulder and his voice softened. "If that's what you're worried about... he's not here."

A soft exhalation left my mouth, though I wasn't sure if it was from relief or disappointment. "That's okay. I'm actually here to go through some of Dad's old things. Would you happen to have a key?"

"Of course. Follow me."

I trailed behind as Carter retrieved a key ring from his desk drawer, then led me to Dad's office. I kept my gaze fixed firmly on the heavy oak door, refusing to let it stray one door down. Was he still at his cabin? Was he doing okay? He'd looked so defeated the last time I saw him and, though I knew he deserved it, I couldn't help but feel bad. I hated that he was hurting—we'd both experienced enough of that.

Carter unlocked the door and held it wide as he flipped on the lights. "Let me know if you need anything."

Sincerity rang in his voice, and I shot him a grateful smile. "I really appreciate it. Thank you."

After Carter left, I closed and locked the door. My eyes skimmed the square room, taking in every detail. The desk was new, barely used, and all of the books, papers, and files were perfectly in place. My fingers trailed over the wood of the desk as I rounded it. How many times had my father sat right here working on business models and architectural plans? I desperately hoped his last months had been good to him.

Two pictures sat on the desk; one was of Dad and me, taken after my wedding. I remembered Jack taking the photo, saying it was a momentous occasion I'd treasure forever. With no family of his own, he knew how important it was to have people that cared. The other picture had been taken in front of Dad's cabin. His arm was looped around Jack's shoulders, and both wore identical grins—just like a father and son.

My heart constricted as I sank into the chair, unable to hold the pain in any longer. The tears came then, hard and fast, and cried until I had nothing left. Exhausted, overwhelmed by guilt and sadness, I laid my head on the desk and allowed sleep to claim me.

SIX

Mia

Silverware clinked against the porcelain of the plates, and I considered how happy I was. For the past two days since he'd come home, we'd spent every waking moment together. We made love, ate, then made love some more. It'd been absolute perfection. It wasn't fair that he'd been gone for so long. Thankfully, that was over. From now on, he'd be here with me—always.

As if sensing my thoughts, Jack glanced across the table and smiled at me. My insides warmed, and an answering smile curved my face. There was nothing sweeter than the sight of him. He'd been a constant in my life for so long, and I loved him so much.

I set the fork on the edge of my plate. "So, I've been taking a photography class this semester."

"Really?" A gorgeous smile lit up his face. "That's awesome."

I felt like a little girl trying to win his approval, and a warm blush crept up my cheeks. I'd known him for years, but this seemed different somehow. I felt nervous and on edge, though I didn't know exactly why. We'd made love several times, but we hadn't spoken much, like we were afraid words would disrupt the blanket of contentment that had settled over us since he'd come home. Maybe it was because we'd been apart for so long. Our bodies knew how to interact, but neither of us knew what to say. He didn't like to talk about his time overseas, so I'd stopped asking. I was sure things would fall into an easy rhythm once he'd had a chance to settle in.

I nodded. "The instructor says I'm pretty good. I can show you some pictures if you want."

"I'd love to see." He studied me for a second. "I'm really glad you're enjoying yourself." He reached across the table and picked up my hand, stroking the back of it with his thumb. The happiness in his expression bled away, replaced by regret. "Sweetheart, there's something I need to talk to you about."

Oh, God. I knew that look.

My breathing turned shallow, and I pulled my hand from his grasp, tucking it in close to my chest. "What's that?"

His mouth twisted. "I know we talked about me being done after this tour, but... they made me a really great offer, and I couldn't turn it down."

My heart froze midbeat. *No.* This couldn't be happening. "You're going back?"

"It's a really great opportunity. It'll be good for us," he insisted. "The money's great, and it's only a yearlong tour. Plus, I'll be there as a civilian, so it's not like I'll be in combat."

I pushed away from the table and glanced out over the backyard. Spring had technically already come and gone, but the trees and flowers hadn't yet begun to bloom. Everything still looked dead, wiped away by a harsh, cold winter. I couldn't believe he was doing this to me.

My words came out flat and emotionless, as lifeless as the flowers outside. "You were supposed to be done."

"I know, sweetheart, but—"

I whirled toward him, anger raising my voice several octaves. "You promised!"

"Mia, honey." His voice was heartbreakingly vulnerable. "I don't want to be away from you, but—"

"Then don't!" Tears sprang to my eyes, and I swiped angrily at them. Why was he doing this? It seemed like he always had an excuse to go running right back to the Army. Didn't he want to be with me anymore? "This is where you belong. Stay with me. Please." I knew I was begging, but I couldn't help it.

He took a deep breath as if trying to rein in his temper. "Can we just talk about this?"

His forced calm, like I was overreacting, only made me madder. "This isn't talking," I snapped. "This is you telling me you're leaving. Again."

"I'm trying to explain." His eyes flashed with aggravation, and I bristled at the borderline condescending tone. "It's a great offer, Mia. You of all people should understand."

"You think I don't understand?" More than anything, I hated being talked down to, and I bristled. "You're right, I don't. I don't know why this is so important to you. Can't you just stay here? You know Daddy will give you any job you want."

Jack was already shaking his head before I finished speaking. "I need to do this. For me, for us."

"So you'd rather be away from me for another year? Then what? That one-year tour will turn into three years. Do you think they'll stop needing you after that? Or will there be another tour, another town or country that needs you?" My breath left my lungs in ragged pants. "What about me?"

He stared at me, seeming to choose his words carefully. "I'm not doing this to be a hero, Mia. These people need help. Without us, they have nothing—"

"I have nothing, Jack." Tears coursed down my cheeks. "All I have is you!"

He looked pained. "I thought you were having fun with your classes?"

To hell with my classes. I'd been taking a couple different courses at the local college, but nothing had really sparked my interest except the photography. My friends had all pretty much moved on and didn't even bother to invite me out anymore. While Jack was off playing soldier, I stayed at home and counted down the days until we could be together again. All I'd ever wanted was him, but the Army was apparently more important to him than his own wife.

I wanted to enjoy life again; I wanted to be happy. I wanted things to go back to the way they were. Why couldn't he understand that? No matter what I did during the day, I still came home to an empty bed at night. It was cold and lonely, and I was sick of it.

Suddenly, I wanted to lash out at him, to hurt him as

badly as he'd hurt me. "Do you know what it's like for me without you here, to be by myself all time?" I propped my hands on my hips and glared at him. "I sit here alone every night while my friends go out and party and have fun."

His body went completely still. "Is that what you want?"

"Why not?" I challenged. "May as well enjoy myself. I can't sit around and wait for you forever."

"Fucking perfect." His face twisted into a sneer as he shook his head. "That's just what a guy wants to hear. That his wife wants to go out to bars and clubs, grind up on other guys. Are you fucking kidding me, Mia?" His voice grew louder and louder with each word until he was yelling, his face red.

"That's not..." I held up my hand as if to slow the conversation that was rapidly spiraling out of control. "I didn't mean it like that."

"Sure as fuck sounded like it." He shoved away from the table. "I can't be here right now."

"You can't just walk away from me!" Fury and apprehension welled inside me.

"I sure as fuck can. You're the one who wants out."

"Fine!" Anger bubbled up and exploded before I could stop it. "Do what you do best, Jack. Leave. If you walk out that door, don't bother to come back."

He leveled a loathing look on me. "Why would I spend one more second with you?"

SEVEN

Mia

My body jerked awake, the memory washing over me as if it had happened yesterday.

Oh, God. Shame rooted me to the seat of the chair. *Oh God, oh God, oh God.*

I'd been so blind, so stupid—it hadn't been him at all. It was me. Eight years ago, I was a selfish, spoiled little girl, and it took losing the love of my life for me to realize that.

After our fight that day, I never saw him again. Furious, I'd waited every day for him to come home and apologize. But he never did. The days passed and turned into weeks, and I knew from talking to my father that Jack had shipped out again. The knowledge that he'd left without saying goodbye stung, and it only served to heighten my anger.

Determined to call his bluff, I contacted a lawyer and had him draw up papers to dissolve the marriage. I was sure when Jack saw them, he'd realize what he was missing. Just over a month after Jack walked out of our house the last time, I dropped the papers in the mail. Barely four weeks later, I got them back. He'd signed them.

I couldn't believe it—he'd let me go, like what we had together meant nothing. A shroud of depression had settled over me. I locked myself in the house and refused to go anywhere. Getting out of bed each day was painful, and sometimes I couldn't even manage. It was almost crippling in its intensity. I even dropped all of my college courses.

The only thing that gave me joy was photography. As spring bled into summer, I occasionally went outside to shoot the colorful new buds on the trees and bushes. It was cathartic, almost, to see the evolution of the plants, how they changed and grew every day. They were resilient—even beaten down by winter, they came back every year, stronger and more vibrant.

After nearly a month, I finally managed to break free of my spell. Without Jack, I couldn't stand to be alone in our home anymore. I couldn't look at his things every day and imagine life without him. I needed to get away from the memories, away from the sadness. Dad tried to talk to me more than once, but I shut him down each time, and finally I stopped speaking with him too.

I withdrew a substantial sum of money from my savings account and put a down payment on an apartment in Seattle. Away from Spokane, away from the memories of the life Jack and I had once shared, I slowly began to move on. What had once begun as anger and a way to punish Jack slowly bled away to sadness and regret. By the time I realized my mistake, it was too late. I'd been waiting for him to apologize and beg for forgiveness, but he never had. Then I'd realized I'd missed one crucial thing—neither had I.

I'd wanted him to accept responsibility and be accountable, but I'd accepted none of it myself. At the time, I felt justified. I thought by giving him the ultimatum, he'd be forced to choose me. But I was wrong. He gave me exactly what he thought I wanted—freedom. I could have gone out with my friends, but I'd chosen not to out of deference to Jack. I didn't care about going to bars and clubs, not really. What irked me the most was the idea of being alone when Jack could and *should*—or so I thought—have been there with me.

Part of what I'd said back then was the truth—without him, I felt cold and empty. I wanted to be the center of his world, just as he was mine. And at twenty-one, it seemed so incredibly unfair that he wasn't around ten months out of the year. I felt like he was letting me down by not being around. Part of me thought I was missing out on something —but the only thing I missed was my marriage, the connection to the one person who'd truly loved me.

I'd been immature and so incredibly selfish, refusing to see that he was truly making a difference in the world—both in the military and for us to have a better life. It was exactly as Jack said: he was doing it for us. He'd never wanted my father's charity. It was precisely the reason he'd enlisted as soon as he'd turned eighteen. Coming from nothing, he was determined to make a life for himself—for us—on his own. I hadn't understood until later how important that was to him.

By the time I realized what I'd done, too much time and distance had grown between us, and I couldn't take back the words I'd said. It got harder and harder to admit that I'd been wrong, so I swallowed my insecurities and tried to move on. But he was always there in the back of my mind, dictating every decision over the past eight years. My heart broke all over again. I'd been so stupid to let him go.

His actions over the last week made perfect sense now.

He'd tried time and again to hold me at bay, and he tried to tell me in his own way that he loved me and still wanted me. He'd never stopped. Everything he'd done had been to protect me—from the threat at Briarleigh and from myself. All along he'd been trying to do the right thing, but I'd been blind to it.

I needed to make amends—right now. I jumped from the chair and threw the door open, quickly glancing around. Hope surged in my chest as I saw the door to his office standing wide open, the light glowing inside. Practically sprinting down the hallway in my haste to see him, I barreled through the doorway—and almost right into a woman.

"Oh! I'm so sorry." Catching myself on the doorframe, I stepped back and smoothed one hand down my shirt. "Have you seen Jack, by chance?"

The pretty strawberry blonde rolled her eyes playfully. "I was just looking for him myself. I stopped in to surprise him, but it figures he wouldn't be here."

My gaze swept over her from head to toe. She was about my age and only a couple inches taller, with curves I envied in all the right places. Her peaches-and-cream skin was flawless, her eyes a bright, sparkling blue with the tiniest crinkles at the corners that invited you to laugh along with her. She didn't wear much makeup, but then, she didn't need to. She was beautiful in a girl-next-door kind of way, and jealousy twisted my stomach into a knot.

Who was she? She wore a cornflower blue shirt that served to make her eyes appear brighter and jeans tucked into a pair of low-heeled leather riding boots. She couldn't possibly be an employee, but she was looking for Jack, which meant...

A prickle of unease lifted the hairs at the base of my

neck, but I forced a polite smile. "I'm sorry, I didn't introduce myself. I'm Mia."

"Sara."

As she uttered the syllables, two worlds collided. It hit me suddenly who this woman was and why she was here. Standing in front of me was Jack's girlfriend—my replacement. I couldn't even bring myself to hate the beautiful, sweet woman. A vise tightened around my lungs as I thought of him with Sara and how happy they must be together. She'd shown up to surprise him, and I would only be in the way. I was too late.

"I... Excuse me." Pain radiated through my chest, and I could practically feel my heart splinter as it shattered apart. Slapping one hand over my mouth to stifle the sob threatening to escape, I turned and fled the room. I was only dimly aware of someone calling my name as I rushed through the lodge and out the front doors, my only goal to escape the image of Jack's lover.

EIGHT

Jack

I ran a hand through my hair and blew out a frustrated breath. Maybe it was for the best that I let her go—I'd done enough damage over the past few days. But the sight of the tears streaming down her face as she'd run from the building literally shredded me. I wanted so badly to go after her, but I couldn't bring myself to interfere any more than I already had.

My entire body shaking, overwhelmed by feelings of insecurity and insignificance, my mind was fully on Mia as I made my way toward my office. I stepped into the room and stopped dead at the sight of the beautiful woman before me. Silence stretched between us for several long seconds, and I shifted uncomfortably before forcing a smile. "Sara. What brings you here?"

I hadn't meant for the words to sound like an accusation, but after everything that had happened with Mia, I wasn't ready for another altercation just yet. Not that Sara would fight me—no, she was much too docile for that. Sara was eternally optimistic and took everything in stride. I'd had second thoughts before, of course, but now... There was no way I could make a life with her.

A tiny smile curled her lips but didn't reach her eyes. "I hadn't heard from you, so I thought I'd stop in."

Guilt assailed me. "I'm sorry I didn't respond to your message. I..."

Truth was, I'd forgotten all about her. I'd been so focused on Mia that I hadn't even taken two minutes out of the day to call or text Sara. She deserved so much more than a guy like me. I opened my mouth to speak, but she shook her head.

"It's okay. I understand." She wandered the office for a moment, examining the pictures on the walls before turning back to me and meeting my gaze. "This place is beautiful. Your description didn't do it justice."

"Thanks."

Sara's next words caught me off guard. "That's her, isn't it?"

Suddenly it all made sense—Sara's reticence, Mia leaving in tears. They must have run into each other. *Oh, God.* I sucked in a sharp breath, desperately trying to ignore the stabbing pain in my heart. Guilt and shame slammed into me. I'd failed both of them. Unable to look away from her, I nodded. "Yes."

"She's beautiful. And she seems very sweet."

I couldn't help the mirthless chuckle that fell from my lips. "You clearly haven't known her long."

"Maybe not." Sara smiled, but just like my laugh, it held no trace of humor. "But I'm a woman. I can tell these things."

She studied me for a long moment. "You really love her, don't you?"

I nodded, unable to bring myself to speak. Discussing my ex-wife with my soon-to-be-ex-lover wasn't exactly something I wanted to do—ever.

"Are you back together?"

There was no hope in her voice, only disappointed acceptance, and it made my heart clench. I'd never wanted to hurt her, but I couldn't bring myself to lie. No matter what happened between Mia and me, things could never go back to the way they were. "Things are... complicated."

She offered up another sad smile that didn't quite reach her eyes. "She loves you."

I swallowed hard. "I think you're mistaken."

"I saw the look in her eyes when she saw me."

"It's not that easy." I pinned my gaze over her shoulder, unable to look at her.

"Love never is." I opened my mouth to refute her statement, but Sara lifted a hand to stop me. "We were never meant to be, Jack. What was between us was easy and fun, and I love you—but not like that." She pointed in the general direction Mia had fled. "Not like her."

My throat constricted, my entire body tensing with the will to control my emotions. If she only knew...

"Jack." Sara's soft voice cut through my tumultuous thoughts. "Whatever happened—it's in the past. That's the kind of love that lasts forever—the kind worth fighting for."

"We'll see." My words came out gruff and curt, eager to end the conversation.

Sara seemed to pick up on my unease, because forced a smile then scooped up the purse she'd set on my desk. "I should be going. It was good to see you." Lifting onto her toes, she dropped a kiss on my cheek and headed for the door. She paused in the doorway and tossed a look over her shoulder at me. "You called for her, you know."

My eyebrows knitted together in confusion, and Sara blushed. Voice pitched low, she said, "When we were... you know. You called out her name."

Jesus. Did I hurt everyone I was close to? I almost choked on the emotion clogging my throat. "I'm sorry. You deserve better."

Another bittersweet smile lifted the corners of her mouth. "And so do you."

As she left my office, I knew without a doubt it would be the last time I saw her. But her words lingered long after she was gone. *That's the kind of love that lasts forever—the kind worth fighting for.*

Loving Mia had been both the easiest and the hardest thing I've ever done. I knew the moment I met her that she was special; with the age difference between us, I'd initially chalked it up to a kinship of sorts. But our mutual attraction had become harder and harder to ignore as the years passed. Our love hadn't diminished with time—it'd grown stronger.

I considered Mia's reaction today. I understood her anger, but why the tears? She wouldn't be sad if she didn't care, right? If I'd learned anything over the past few days, it was that I loved her more than I had ten years ago. I needed to fight for her this time around. I wasn't going to just let her walk away again—not when I knew she loved me, too.

My lips kicked into a wry smile as I sank into my chair. I also knew Mia, and she'd definitely need a day or two to come around. The woman was too damn stubborn, but that's what I loved most about her. I'd give her some time to cool off, then I would set everything right. I'd spill the truth and tell her exactly how I felt. It wasn't going to be an easy road, but I'd walk through hell for her if I had to. There was always the possibility that she'd shoot me down again, just as she had eight years ago. A lump formed in my throat at the thought, and I ruthlessly pushed the negative emotions away. No matter what happened, I wanted Mia to be happy.

My phone rang, distracting me from my morose thoughts, and I lifted it to my ear with barely a glance at the screen. "What do you have for me?"

Donahue snorted on the other end of the line. "I like how you make it sound as if I'm at your beck and call."

I remained silent. Thankfully the sheriff picked up on the subtle nuance and continued without having to be prompted. "It took some doing, but we pulled up her car."

My heart skipped a beat, the news propelling me forward in my chair. "And?"

"It's gonna take a while, but my team will look it over for any evidence. You know, though..."

I let out a sigh as Donahue trailed off. Yeah, I knew. The weather would've likely obliterated anything left at the scene. Still, it was worth a shot. "All we need is a lead."

"We're bringing Brown in for questioning."

Rage simmered in my blood. "You think he's responsible for Mia's accident?"

Toby Brown had been a thorn in my side since the day Bruce and I bought the foreclosed property. The land Briarleigh and our respective cabins sat on had belonged to Toby's family for generations. We'd tried to make amends with him, but Toby wanted nothing to do with it. He'd rather carry a grudge than see reason. I couldn't help feeling bad for the guy, but if he'd hurt Mia...

"I've got two deputies on the hunt for him right now, so I'll let you know once I have something more conclusive. I'd like to say he's not that stupid, but..."

I scowled. If the man felt threatened enough, anything was possible.

"There's something else. We found some building materials behind Ol' Smokey. Think they might be yours." Ol' Smokey, as it had been dubbed, was a dilapidated old mill that hadn't been in use for decades. Now a crumbling pile of bricks, it was widely used as a dump site. It was illegal, but most people didn't care. Up here, it was it was usually the cheapest and easiest way to get rid of stuff. "One of the folks in town came forward—"

I blinked at that. Who the hell would've risked getting fined just to relay some information, especially about a ski lodge half the town resented? I'd made friends with the right people in the hopes of paving the way for an easy transition for both myself and the people of Pine Ridge, but I wasn't an idiot. Some of them—like Toby Brown—would never see it as anything but an infringement on their small town.

"—and said he saw some lumber down there, some spools of wiring. Sound familiar?"

I rolled my eyes. "Sure does."

"Even if he says he had nothing to do with Mia's accident, maybe we can get enough to stick."

"If it's him, I don't want to press charges. Unless, of course, he's the one behind her accident." Though, really, it hadn't been an accident at all. We both knew that.

"Jack..."

I waved off the concern in Donahue's voice. "I know what you're going to say. It's not his fault they lost the land. But he needs to know this is the last warning."

"You know it's not just up to you now."

I picked up a pen lying on the desk and twirled it between my fingers. "I know, I just..."

"This isn't something you can keep from her."

I scowled. "I'm not trying to keep it from her. I just don't want her involved with him. At all."

Honestly, I was beginning to doubt that Toby had anything to do with Mia's disappearance. The man was a troublemaker, but he'd never physically hurt anyone. The embezzling had been going on for a while but had stopped almost as soon as Mia arrived. Brent and Janine stood to gain partial control of the company if Mia didn't uphold her part of the bargain. What only a few people knew, though, was that I already had it set in motion to roll my share over to her once building was complete. Had they somehow found out? Maybe they hoped that if she was completely out of the picture, they would receive the remaining shares.

Anger surged through me. They would bear watching. Janine hadn't been here at the time of the break-in and Mia's accident, but Brent had. He was Bruce's stepson, after all. What if he'd somehow gotten access to the files and started skimming off the top?

I turned my attention back to Donahue. "I think we need to look more closely at McCann. He was here with her the first two days, then she and her stuff magically disappeared. He's one of the few people—besides my crew—who had access to that kind of information."

I'd need to look deeper into our crew again, keep my ear to the ground and see if there were any stirrings of unrest. Carter would probably know better than I would. I made a mental note to check with him when I hung up.

"I'll take care of it." Donahue's voice filtered through the line. "Just keep an eye on her, make sure she's safe until I get some answers."

My lips twisted into a grim smile. I'd been doing that for years. I wouldn't know how to stop if I wanted to.

NINE

Mia

I stared listlessly out the window, watching the snowflakes swirl in a dance through the early morning air. It would make a pretty picture, but I couldn't summon the enthusiasm or the energy to peel myself off the couch. I hadn't made it to bed last night, crashing here on the couch instead, sobbing into the throw pillows in the corner. I dozed off and on, but I'd been awake when the first gray light of dawn broke over the horizon.

I hated feeling pathetic and sad, but I couldn't help it. I'd messed everything up. Again. Bella placed her head in my lap and nudged my hand, coaxing a small smile from me. It was amazing, really, how the dog seemed intuitive to my feelings. She always knew the exact moment to give me a slight nudge or do something silly to make me laugh. She'd been my lifeline over the past few days since I'd left Jack's house.

I scratched her ears as she nuzzled against me. "Do you

need to go outside?" She danced backward, tail wagging furiously, and I couldn't help but laugh. "All right, let's go."

I pushed up from the couch and headed to the foyer to bundle up. Ears perked up, Bella trembled with excitement at the prospect of going outside. Fresh air would do me good, hopefully pull me out of my funk, at least for a few minutes. Determined not to wallow in my own pity—not to mention my stupidity—I slipped into the heavy coat Jack had bought me and tugged on my gloves. The only other time I'd worn them was when we'd hiked down the mountain to try to find my car. The rest of the time had been spent inside the cabin.

Everything reminded me of him, and another pang of sadness ricocheted through my heart. Shoving it down, I stepped into my boots and opened the door. Outside, the sounds of the woods greeted us. Birds sang, and small animals chattered in the trees. One particularly brave squirrel stopped in front of the porch and tipped its head at Bella, a string of high-pitched squeaks leaving its mouth.

Before I could blink, Bella tore past me, giving chase. "Bella, no!"

They were out of sight by the time I hit the bottom step, and my heart jumped into my throat. *Oh, God.* What if she got lost, or worse? What if she was hurt out here? There were mountain lions and moose, not to mention bears. If she ran into a mama with a cub...

Panicked, I took off after them, following Bella's excited barks. Several minutes later, I found them. Bella stood on her hind legs, her front paws placed on the tree as she barked up at the squirrel, who chattered back indignantly.

Winded but thankful I'd found her, I rested my hands on my knees and took several deep breaths. "Come on, Bells, let's get home." The dog threw me a disgruntled look before glancing back up the tree at the cornered squirrel. "Bella." I put as much warning into my tone as possible, and the dog reluctantly dropped to all fours.

"Good girl." I patted her head as she came and leaned against my legs. I threw a look at the squirrel. "Don't tease her next time and you won't get chased."

The squirrel sat there, silent, a blank look on its face. *Great. I'm talking to animals now.*

I shook my head and turned to head for the cabin. We took our time on the way back, Bella stopping to sniff every tree. She dashed through the snow, kicking up the powdery flakes, chasing her tail and making me laugh. "Come on, you big goofball."

Back inside, I shed my heavy gear and felt the shroud of sadness descend over me once more. I needed to do something, but what? Needing to keep my hands busy, I headed to the coffeepot. I dumped the cold liquid that remained from this morning and started a fresh brew. Several minutes later, with a cup of warm coffee in my hands, I settled back into the corner of the couch.

I was still angry that Jack hadn't told me the truth, but I no longer blamed him. He'd done everything in his power to keep me safe, and I trusted him with my life. He'd tried so hard to resist, too. I'd practically thrown myself at him before he'd given in to the desire crackling between us.

It had always been that way, and I knew it always would. I'd been such a brat when I was younger. I'd thrown away the best thing to ever happen to me because I was selfish and self-centered. I wanted all or nothing. Unfortunately, life didn't always work that way. He'd done what he thought was best at the time—I just hadn't wanted to acknowledge it. Yes, he should have discussed it with me first, but I was sure my answer at the time wouldn't have changed.

If I were in Jack's shoes, I wouldn't have told me either. He probably expected me to pitch a fit and demand to leave. And a year ago, I would have. Hell, even a month ago I would've shut him down. But Dad's death had opened my eyes to a lot of things I didn't necessarily want to see about myself. The question was, where did we go from here? Was there even a *we* anymore?

The phone buzzed on the coffee table, and I turned my head to glance at it. Probably Brent again. He'd been calling a couple times a day to make sure I was okay. I appreciated it, but it was tiresome. I wanted to wallow in pity alone until my heart didn't feel as if it'd been shattered beyond repair. Unfortunately, I wasn't sure it would ever feel better.

Eric Donahue's name lit the screen, and I reluctantly answered. "Hello?"

I heard rustling and a low din in the background before he responded. "Mia, it's Sheriff Donahue. I wanted to fill you in on a couple things."

Eric relayed the information he'd received regarding Toby Brown, the man who'd threatened me at the bar when I'd first arrived. "One of my deputies picked him up at the bar late last night."

I sucked in a breath. "What did he say?"

"Ah," Donahue hesitated. "We haven't had a chance to question him. He was rather... incapacitated."

I rolled my eyes. Figured he was too drunk to talk. To my way of thinking, that's probably when they should have questioned him. Maybe he would've told the truth. "What do you think will happen?"

"If we find sufficient evidence, you can press charges."

I mulled that over. I didn't want to create any more

animosity between the locals. We needed to learn to coexist. "What did Jack say?"

Eric heaved a sigh, as if he didn't want to impart what Jack had told him. "If Toby's responsible, he suggested letting him off with a warning."

My heart warmed. "I agree."

Silence filled the end of the line for a minute. "Are you sure? After everything..."

I shook my head despite the fact he couldn't see me. "I'm sure. But tell him to stay away from me and Jack, otherwise I'm filing a restraining order."

"Okay." The sheriff's voice was deceptively calm. "I'll relay the message."

Before he hung up, I needed to know... "Is Jack with you?"

"Not at the moment, but I'm planning to stop up at Briarleigh in a bit. I have a few things to go over with him." He paused. "Is there something you need?"

"Tell him..." I bit my lip. There was too much that needed to be said, and it needed to be done in person. "Never mind."

"Is everything okay?"

"Fine, fine," I assured him. "It's no big deal."

"Okay." He waited a beat, then, "If you need anything, don't hesitate to ask."

"I will. And thank you."

I hung up and stared at the phone for a minute before setting it down on the coffee table. It would be the height of stupidity to text Jack now. I was sure he was still angry with me, and I didn't know the words to say to make it better. This was going to take a lot of work to fix, and I needed a game plan.

TEN

Jack

I raked one hand through my hair. "What now?"

Donahue sprawled in the chair on the opposite side of the desk and lifted a shoulder. "I'm holding him on principle, but he denies having anything to do with Ms. Hamilton."

Son of a bitch. That was the last thing I wanted to hear, but I couldn't say I hadn't expected it. "Well, isn't there something else we can do?"

Eric sighed. "I have a dozen people saying Toby was at Murdoch's until close to 2:00 a.m. I can fine him for illegal dumping, but other than that..."

I blew out a frustrated breath. "So we're back to square one." My gut twisted into knots, instinct screaming at me. Something still didn't feel right. If Toby wasn't involved, then maybe there was only one person responsible. I should've been focusing on whoever was embezzling the funds instead of chasing Toby and trying to pin the missing materials on him. But at least it was a start. It was an answer we hadn't known before. Now to flush out whoever was involved in the company. Who the hell could it be?

I let out a low growl. "Brent is the only other person who's had any contact with her. When's the last time you talked to him or Mrs. Hamilton?"

"Only right after Mia disappeared. I couldn't keep pestering them without reasonable cause." Donahue lifted a hand, palm up. "Now that Toby's been cleared, though..."

I lifted a brow. "Time to go talk to McCann again?"

"If you're up for it." The sheriff placed his hands on his wide-spread knees and pushed to his feet. "I'm not confident that it'll yield anything but it's worth a try."

I pushed my chair back and stood. "I don't care what I have to do. If it keeps Mia safe, it's worth it."

"But"—Eric slashed a hand through the air—"for the love of God, let me ask the questions."

My lips pressed into a thin line, but Donahue's face remained stoic and impassive, and I finally rolled my eyes. "Fine. But I still think I can get more information out of him."

Donahue chuckled. "Yeah, I can only imagine your interview technique. Seriously, though. Don't blow this." He pointed at me. "And don't make me arrest you."

I barely refrained from rolling my eyes again. The sheriff wouldn't arrest me. I hoped. Either way, talking to Brent again was worth a try. Maybe the man had forgotten some little detail.

I held the door open for Eric as we stepped into the hallway. We were immediately waylaid as Carter approached. "Hey, I'm glad I caught you both."

"What's up?" I tipped my chin at him.

"Remember Mia's ski accident?"

I stared blankly at him. "What are you talking about?"

Carter made a face. "The day before she disappeared? Remember?"

"Obviously not." Brent had said she'd 'taken a fall,' but the way Carter spoke made it sound like a whole hell of a lot more. A sick feeling took up residence in my stomach. "Tell me."

"I had Summer pull inventory, but it kind of got put on the back burner while we got everything else ready for the soft opening. I didn't think much of it at the time, but with everything going on... I should have known." He glanced guiltily at me. "It looks like someone made a partial cut through the plastic, and it snapped the rest of the way when she fell."

I took the U-shaped piece of hard gray plastic from Carter and turned it over in my hands. The binding was designed to attach to the ski and keep the person's boot securely in place. Except, in Mia's case, it hadn't. There was a jagged line where the plastic had cracked, causing her to fall. But at the very edge the cut was distinct and straight, as if someone had taken a knife to it.

Eric and I shared a look. "Definitely need to talk with him now."

I clapped a hand on Carter's shoulder. "Thanks, man. I've got a few things to do, so I doubt I'll be back today."

"Good luck."

I nodded to Carter and followed Eric to the parking lot. "I'll follow you."

Nerves frayed, I followed the sheriff up the winding road to Brent's cabin. Two cars sat in the driveway, and I immediately recognized the little SUV as Brent's. The Mercedes was a new addition, and I rolled my eyes. It could only belong to one person.

Flanking Eric, I stepped onto the porch as he knocked

on the door. It was thrown open seconds later, revealing Brent. Without a word, Mia's stepbrother held the door wide and we stepped inside only to be cornered by Janine.

Her lips curled into a sneer. "Back to antagonize us some more?"

"Nice to see you, Mrs. Hamilton." I intentionally used her married name to drive home her adultery, and her mouth pinched.

Her eyes narrowed before turning her scathing glare on Eric. "Well, to what do we owe this unwelcome visit?"

"Mother," Brent warned.

Eric held up his hands in a placating motion. "We just stopped by to see if you've heard anything on your side, or if you've remembered anything."

Brent heaved a sigh. "No. I can't think of anything else."

"All right." Eric nodded, his gaze sweeping the room. "Would you mind if I took a look around, just in case?"

"Be my guest."

Brent's dry tone implied otherwise, but Eric dipped his head in an appreciative nod. "Thanks. I'll be quick. You guys want to come with me?"

I nodded, and Brent did the same. McCann was probably worried the sheriff would try to pin something on him, and I wanted to be there for backup.

From behind them, Janine's voice piped up. "What are you looking for, Sheriff? Shouldn't you be out doing your job, trying to find out what happened to Amelia?"

The sheriff pulled a pair of nitrile gloves from his back pocket and slipped them on. "That's what we're attempting to do, ma'am."

Eric's voice was way more controlled than I could ever manage. No wonder the sheriff had told me to keep my mouth shut. I'd only been in her presence for a matter of minutes and I was ready to boot her ass out of the house. I gritted my teeth as we made our way through the small cabin, Janine keeping up a running commentary the whole time.

"I just don't understand," she huffed as Eric pushed open the closet doors of the spare bedroom. "What exactly do you think you're going to accomplish here?"

"Well, ma'am, I'm just looking for anything that can help." Eric stiffened, then pulled something down from a high shelf.

"What's..." Janine's words trailed off and she threw a bewildered look at Brent, who looked just as stunned as his mother.

I watched in silent horror as Eric unzipped the blue suitcase to reveal mounds of feminine clothes. He sifted through folds of fabric and finally lifted out a purse. The sheriff glanced at Brent as he pulled Mia's ID from the wallet. "Care to explain?"

Motherfucker. My gaze flew to Mia's stepbrother, and I summoned every ounce of control ingrained in me so I wouldn't rip into him with my bare hands.

"I don't know how... That's not..." Brent stuttered, flustered.

Eric set the purse back in the luggage and stepped toward McCann. "I'm going to need you to come down to the station to answer some questions."

"But I didn't..." He threw an imploring look at Janine. "I didn't do anything!"

Janine fell silent, lips pressed together in a firm line. Finally she held out her hand. "Give me your phone. I'll call our lawyer."

Anger brewed as I watched Brent pass the phone to his

mother, still sputtering. "I swear I had no idea. I don't know where those came from!"

"I'm going to ask you again," Eric said, his tone hard and unforgiving. "You can come willingly, or I'll call for a warrant right now."

Brent held up his hands, like he'd probably seen criminals do on TV. "No, I'll go."

Eric repacked the suitcase and retrieved a second set of gloves, then tossed them to me. "Can you bring this out?"

"No problem." I slipped the gloves on so I wouldn't contaminate any potential fingerprints, then hefted the suitcase.

Eric grasped McCann's upper arm and led him out of the cabin to the cruiser. I watched as Janine silently gathered her things, then slipped into her coat and made her way to the front door. She paused with her hand on the doorknob and glanced over her shoulder at me, her face unreadable.

I opened my mouth to say something, but no words came out. What the hell could I say? Her son was being questioned for burglary, not to mention attempted kidnapping and/or murder. This looked terrible; we all knew it. Whatever emotion had flitted briefly across her features was gone, the insolent mask back in place. I followed her outside, making sure to lock up behind me, then climbed into my Tahoe. Inside, I seethed. How could Brent be so fucking greedy? And stupid? Why the hell would he have stashed Mia's things in his own cabin?

Something didn't make sense. I put the truck in gear and followed the other cars down the mountain, watching as Janine veered off, heading back to the resort instead of following Eric to the Sheriff's Office. As I navigated the winding roads, I replayed the events in my mind. Brent had looked stunned. More than stunned, actually—he'd looked blindsided, like he truly had no idea Mia's things were even in his house. Though the evidence was damn near irrefutable, there was something about Brent's sincerity, the way he'd pleaded for us to believe him...

I sighed. Anyone in McCann's situation would do the same thing. They'd beg and plead and deny the charges until they were caught red-handed. My gut churned, and something niggled at the back of my mind. Brent had all of Mia's things. He had to be the one behind all this... right?

ELEVEN

Mia

Frustration and anxiety curled through me as I stared at my phone. I was so tired of being cooped up, feeling scared and defenseless. On top of that, I still hadn't decided what to do about Jack. I wanted to talk to him, but I was terrified of what he'd say. Would he turn me away or would he hear me out?

I hadn't left the house at all except to let the dog outside to play, but I was tired of avoiding the problem. I needed closure, and I needed to know the truth. The first thing I had to take care of was Brent.

Once more I checked the time and glanced at his message: **Be there soon**.

That'd been nearly forty minutes ago. What the hell was he doing?

Now that my memory had finally resurfaced, I'd begun to contemplate different scenarios. I didn't think Carter Reed had anything to do with the embezzling. Jack seemed to believe Carter, and I trusted his judgment implicitly.

Toby appeared to be a troublemaker, but I personally didn't think he had the knowledge to pull off something this large or complex. Of course, my knowledge of him was based solely on my singular experience with the man and what I'd gleaned from others. According to the bartender, Murdoch, Toby was a blue-collar kind of guy who worked the land and avoided anything technology-based. Eliminating those two left few options.

Brent was good with numbers. Janine had been hostile at the reading of the will and, I thought, maybe angry enough to lash out. What if she and Brent were working together? The thought made my blood boil with fury. I didn't want to believe either of them could be responsible, but I wasn't an idiot; they were the only people who stood to gain anything if I failed to fulfill the stipulations of Dad's will.

My phone buzzed with the arrival of another text, and my lips pressed into a thin line of irritation. So help me, if Brent was blowing me off, I was going to track his ass down. My heart leaped as I saw Jack's name light up the screen.

I'll understand if you don't want to talk. Just need to know you're okay.

Biting my lip, I debated what to say. I wanted to tell him everything. I needed to see him, but I had no idea how he felt. Still, he'd made the effort to reach out to me, and I wouldn't let it pass me by. I quickly typed out a response. **I'm fine.**

Three little dots flickered in the lower corner of the screen. **Good**. Another message followed a few seconds later. **I really am sorry about everything.**

I know. I bit my lip and my fingers flew over the

keyboard, hesitating only briefly before hitting the send button. **I need to talk to you**.

His response was almost immediate. **Any time.**

I let out a sigh of relief, hope surging in my heart. Maybe there was a chance for us after all. As soon as I addressed the issue with Brent, I would pour my heart out the way I should have years ago. I just prayed that he would listen. After seeing Sara yesterday, I had my doubts, but I brushed them away. I had to at least try. **Need to clear the air with Brent. Later, maybe?**

We can deal with him later. Can I come see you?

He wants to see me. My pulse leaped, and a silly grin spread over my face as I hurriedly tapped a message back to him. **Brent's on his way over. Call you later xoxo**

It'd already been three days since I'd left his house, and I was literally counting down the seconds until I would see him again. I couldn't wait to get this over with. I wanted to talk to Brent, then send him on his way.

Bella let out a low growl, and seconds later I heard a vehicle pull into the driveway. *Speak of the devil.* My phone began to ring almost immediately, and I saw Jack's name roll across the screen. I bit my lip before silencing it. He was probably calling to convince me not to confront Brent. But he was my problem, and I was going to put this to rest once and for all.

Setting my phone on the coffee table, I pushed up from the couch and made my way to the front window. As the vehicle drew closer, Bella's growls turned to menacing barks. I petted the dog's head, softly crooning to her. "Shh. It's okay, girl."

The bright midafternoon sun beat down on the windshield of the truck, obscuring my view. I took in the snow-plow on the front and the familiar hunter green Briarleigh logo on the driver door as it rolled up to the house. I didn't recognize the man who stepped out of the truck, but some-thing about his face struck me as vaguely familiar. I'd seen him somewhere before; I was sure of it.

Beside me Bella continued to bark, and my eyes skated over the visitor once more. I knew I recognized his face, but I couldn't place him. Maybe I'd seen him at the lodge. That had to be it. Standing off to the side of the window, I watched him approach the cabin, debating what to do. I didn't think he'd seen me yet, as bright as it was outside. Maybe I should just pretend I wasn't home. As soon as the thought flitted through my brain, I remembered the red rental car parked off to the side, and I mentally rolled my eyes. *Maybe not.*

I chewed on a thumbnail. Being around people still made me uneasy. I had a feeling it would be that way until we figured out who had broken into the cabin and tried to chase me away. I was probably blowing this whole thing out of proportion. It was the middle of the day—the guy was probably just here for some routine maintenance. Besides, I'd promised myself yesterday I was going to put on a brave front. I wouldn't let them see how weak and vulnerable I truly felt.

Still, I didn't trust anyone right now, and I wasn't just going to throw caution to the wind. Brent should be arriving any minute, and I would be safe enough until he got here. I'd see what the man wanted and send him on his way. Mind made up, I turned toward the kitchen and snapped my fingers at the dog. "Come."

She ignored me completely, barking at the stranger like it was her job.

"Bella!" Exasperated, I slipped my fingers beneath her collar and guided her to the pantry. I'd never heard Bella growl like that—so deep and ferocious I could practically feel the hostility rolling off her body in waves. I didn't know much about dogs in general. Maybe she was just being extra protective after the emotional upheaval of leaving Jack's house. I appreciated the gesture, but I was worried she might try to attack the employee from Briarleigh. I used my most soothing voice to put her at ease. "Come on. Everything's fine, girl. You just wait in here."

I closed the door to Bella's whining and went to answer the door. My phone vibrated on the coffee table and I knew it was probably Jack calling—again.

If I let him, he would swoop in and try to be my knight in shining armor. Part of me wanted to give in and let him. I wanted him to do what he did best—make everything better. He'd always taken care of me, but that was half the problem. I was an expert at sweeping things under the rug so I didn't have to deal with them, and that was exactly what had landed me in this position in the first place. I'd allowed my bitterness to drive away my husband, then my father. It was time for me to address my own problems—starting with Brent. He was my cross to bear, and I needed to deal with him head-on. If Brent really had done all these awful things, I needed to ask him why face-to-face. He owed me that much, at least.

I opened the door, praying that the employee would quickly be on his way. I didn't want an audience when I had my heart-to-heart with Brent.

The man stood on the porch, dressed in overalls and a thick hunter-green parka, the Briarleigh logo emblazoned in white across his chest. He offered me a smile. "Good afternoon, miss."

I studied him as he spoke. He was handsome, though not overtly so. On first sight, his features appeared nondescript. The longer I looked at him, though, the more I noticed the sharp gray eyes, high cheekbones, and long, aquiline nose. Why did he look so familiar?

A skitter of unease slithered down my spine. Something about him set me on edge. I shook it off, chalking it up to the events of the past couple weeks. Memories of the break-in and my accident plagued me, and I had a feeling I'd be wary of strangers for a while. I glanced past him once more to the truck in the driveway. Had Jack sent him up here to check on me? Maybe that's why he'd been calling. The timing was eerily coincidental, and I couldn't dismiss it outright despite the niggle of worry at the base of my neck.

I returned the man's polite smile. "Can I help you?"

"Hello, miss. My name's Kenneth. I work down at Briarleigh." He gestured with his thumb over his shoulder in the general direction of the lodge. "I just wanted to stop in and make sure everything's okay for you."

It wasn't an unreasonable request, and yet... "Are you looking for something in particular?"

"During the winter season, we like to check the generators every few weeks or so. We run them when the power goes out so the pipes won't freeze," Kenneth explained.

I let out a short laugh, feeling completely ridiculous. "I actually meant to ask Carter about it the other day, but I completely forgot. I'm kind of surprised the pipes didn't burst last week when the power went out."

The man just smiled benignly. "We try to keep up with the cabins in the outlying areas, checking routinely so that doesn't happen."

"I appreciate it." I smiled at him. Bella's barking grew

increasingly frantic, and I could hear the dog scratching at the pantry door.

The man threw me when he changed subjects completely. "If you don't mind my asking, miss, I was just wondering how you like it so far. Are you planning to stay?"

Bewilderment made me blink. Was he being nice, or was he hitting on me? My gaze skimmed over his features again. It was difficult to tell exactly how old he was, but he was probably fifteen years older than me, if not more. He was handsome enough, but he did nothing for me. There was only one man I wanted, but I had no idea if Jack felt the same. What would I do if he pushed me away? I didn't want to think about it. Life had been lonely before, but now, remembering what it was like to be in his arms... What would I do without him?

Despair settled over me and I tamped it down so Kenneth wouldn't see my rioting emotions. Affecting a neutral expression, I lifted one shoulder. "It's really beautiful, but I doubt I'll be here long-term."

He nodded as if he understood, his penetrating gaze fixed on mine. "Sorry to hear that."

The corners of my mouth lifted in a tight smile, but Kenneth remained on the porch. My phone continued to vibrate on the table, and Bella's barking echoed in my ears. Suddenly it was all too much. I needed to deal with Jack, then the dog. "Excuse me, I should get that. If I can help with anything, just let me know."

I started to shut the door, but he stopped me with a palm on the wood. "Don't."

The single word froze me in my tracks. "I'm sorry?"

Steel-gray eyes piercing mine, he tipped his chin toward my phone. "Don't answer that."

Apprehension snaked down my spine and I fought the urge to shiver under his intense scrutiny. I grabbed at the only lifeline I had, hoping it would deter him from whatever game he was playing. "I'm expecting someone soon." I chanced a glance out the window, praying for a glimpse of Brent's SUV. Where the hell was he? *Damn it, Brent, hurry up.* "He should be here any minute, in fact."

The man lifted a brow. "Looking for Brent?"

My gaze jumped back to him, and my breath caught. "How...?"

Slowly, the man pulled something flat and rectangular from the pocket of his parka. "He's not coming."

I shook my head. "I just talked with him, he—"

"Brent didn't text you." Kenneth stepped over the threshold, and I automatically stepped backward to maintain a healthy distance between us.

My mind felt sluggishly slow as I fought to understand what he was saying.

"I did." The look in his eyes turned dark and intense as he extended the black object toward me. "Brent's not coming."

My breath caught as I finally understood what I was looking at. *Brent's phone.*

I took another step backward as he advanced into the room. My mind whirled, caught between the need to defend myself and the need to call for help. Grab a knife from the kitchen or go for my phone? Jack would know what to do, but how long would it take him to get here?

Oh, God.

My heart dropped to my toes as Kenneth pulled a pistol from his waistband. "Don't be stupid, Amelia."

Bella's barking grew increasingly louder and more frantic, the scratching sound intensifying as she clawed at the wood.

Kenneth raised the pistol and pointed it at me. "You're going to do exactly as I say. Understand?"

Fear crawled up my throat, choking me, but I managed to nod. Maybe if I played along, I could get outside and make a break for it.

"Good girl. Now—"

Suddenly there was an explosion of sound behind me as the pantry door splintered and cracked. I glanced over my shoulder to see Bella launching herself through the hole in the door with a ferocious growl.

The report of gunfire filled the air, and I sank to my knees, a silent scream suspended in my throat.

TWELVE

Jack

I palmed my phone, restlessly turning it over and over, needing something to keep my hands busy. I glanced through the two-way glass of the interview room again where Sheriff Donahue leaned a hip against the steel table. The sheriff had questioned Brent extensively for the past half hour, but, so far, McCann had vehemently denied everything. The hell of it was, I believed him.

Brent's initial reaction and every statement since seemed completely sincere. Either he was the best fucking actor in the world or he truly had nothing to do with Mia's disappearance.

I scrubbed a hand over my face. Fuck, I had to talk to her. This rift between us was just too much. At the very least, I needed to know she was okay. I stared at the phone, wavering between the overwhelming desire to hear her voice and the fear that she'd once again turn me away. My thumb hovered over the number, yet I couldn't bring myself to dial, terrified that her voice would hold the disdain I so rightly deserved.

Tapping back to the main screen, I brought up my messages and began to type. **I'll understand if you don't want to talk. Just need to know you're okay.**

I quickly hit the green button to send the message before I could second-guess myself. Drawing in a sharp breath, I closed my eyes briefly before returning my gaze to the interview room.

Eric loomed over the table, speaking with a terrified-looking Brent. The evidence was damning, but something niggled at the back of my brain. This didn't jive. Something was wrong; I just couldn't figure out what it was.

Brent looked sincere as he gave Eric his answers, denying any involvement in hurting Mia. Yet he had her things. Why... how?

My phone buzzed, and my breath caught as I saw Mia's name flash across the screen. **I'm fine**

It was short and succinct, but not abrupt. I decided to test the waters. **Good**.

Shit. That wasn't enough. I wanted to keep her going, but I struggled for something to say. Only one thing came to mind, and I figured it was as good as anything. **I really am sorry about everything.**

I held my breath as three little dots appeared, followed almost immediately by an incoming message.

I know.

My lips pressed into a thin line as I stared at the screen. What the hell did that mean?

I need to talk to you

Her response stunned me, and my heart galloped in my chest. Typically those were words I never wanted to hear, but at least she was speaking to me now. I'd take whatever the hell I could get. I didn't hesitate to send a message back. **Any time.**

Need to clear the air with Brent. Later, maybe?

Fuck her talking with Brent. I had no idea how much she knew, but I didn't want her to know of his possible betrayal. If anyone was going to break it to her, it was going to be me. But not until we addressed whatever the hell was going on between us. **We can deal with that later. Can I come see you?**

It was really a cursory question—I was going to see her whether she wanted me to or not. These past few days had damn near killed me, and I couldn't stand to be away from her for one more second. I'd rather be getting reamed by her than on the receiving end of her silent treatment. I rapped my knuckles on the two-way glass to get Eric's attention.

The door opened and Eric's head peeked out. "Whatcha need?"

I tipped my chin at the sheriff. "I'm headed up to Mia's. Keep me posted."

The buzzing of the phone in my hand drew my attention back to our messages, and my brow furrowed as I read her words. **Brent's on his way over. Call you later xoxo**

My heart leaped at the "xoxo" she'd tacked on, and it took several seconds for the other words to sink in. I lifted my gaze to Eric. "Did McCann say anything about going to see Mia today?"

The sheriff shook his head. "Not that I'm aware of. Why?"

I pushed past him and strode into the interview room. Brent's eyes were full of fear as they landed on me.

"Prescott—"

I ignored Eric's warning, my attention focused completely on Brent. "Did you tell Mia you were coming to see her today?"

He shook his head. "No. I've texted her a few times, but she said she wanted her space."

My mind spun as I worked out scenarios, none of them good. "Does your mom still have your phone?"

He shrugged. "She was going to call my lawyer." His expression turned tentative. "Why? What's going on?"

Fear slithered down my spine. "Someone told Mia they're coming to see her. And she thinks it's you." I remembered that look Janine had shot me just before leaving Brent's cabin. I hadn't understood it at the time, but was that resignation I'd seen in her eyes? Had greed made her do the unthinkable: set up her own son to take the fall? "You said your mom was the last person to have your phone?"

"Yes, I..." His words trailed off, and his face took on a deathly hue. "Oh, God. *No*. She wouldn't..."

My mouth pressed into a grim line. If Brent wasn't responsible, the only other person who stood to gain from Mia's demise was Janine. "She's the last person to have had your phone. If Mia doesn't fulfill the stipulations..." I trailed off, allowing the implication to sink in.

"Oh, God. I'm going to be sick." Brent's complexion turned a sickly pale shade and Eric rushed to grab a small trash can sitting outside the interview room. He passed it to Brent, who immediately bent at the waist and retched.

I whipped toward Eric. "I've gotta go."

With a curt nod, the sheriff warned, "Don't do anything stupid."

"No promises." I took off at a fast clip, and the sound of the sheriff's voice calling for cleanup dissipated as I pushed through the door and took off at a jog across the parking lot. The cold air assaulted me, spurring me on.

I hopped into the SUV and sped up the mountain, fifteen miles per hour over the speed limit. As I drove, I dug my phone from my back pocket. One eye on the road, I tapped Carter's number and waited for it to connect.

"Hey, boss."

"I need a favor."

"Shoot."

I fought to keep the Tahoe between the lines as I raced toward Mia's place. "The employee that Janine was seen with, do you know who it was?"

"I didn't see them personally," Carter said slowly, "but I can see if anyone else has."

"Do that. I need to know ASAP."

"I'll see what I can do. Any reason in particular?"

I hesitated for a moment before responding. I hated to keep Carter in the dark about this, but I didn't want to drag anyone else into our mess. "Someone texted Mia from Brent's phone that they're on their way over."

"Are you positive it's not—" Disbelief colored Carter's voice and I cut in.

"Donahue's got Brent in lockup down at the SO. I need to know who the hell we're dealing with."

Carter sucked in a breath. "Christ. Give me a couple minutes and I'll see what I can dig up."

I cut the call and dropped the phone to my lap as the trees flew by in a green blur. My agitation grew with each mile. I was only about ten miles out now, but I was at least a good half hour behind whoever was headed to Mia's. The thought of her accident a couple weeks back made me see red. Someone obviously wanted to get rid of Mia by whatever means necessary—and I'd be damned if I was going to let it happen.

My phone rang, and I snatched it up. "Talk to me."

"I have two guys here that say Mrs. Hamilton has been seen with Mac. HR is sending his file now, so..." He trailed off midsentence. "Hang on, it just came through."

I curled my fingers around the wheel, anxiety and frustration pulsing through me. Who the hell was Mac? I couldn't recall a face off the top of my head, but he had to have some kind of connection to Janine. I seriously doubted she'd jumped into bed with the guy as soon as she'd arrived at Briarleigh, though I couldn't dismiss the possibility outright. It was more likely they'd been working together for some time now, but how long? And, maybe the better question—why?

"I've got it in front of me now." Carter's voice was distracted, and I imagined him skimming the man's dossier. "He started working for Hamilton a couple years ago, doing janitorial work back in Spokane before making the jump to Briarleigh. He now takes care of the grounds here, operates the plow, that kind of thing."

Irritation pulled at me. I didn't give a shit about the guy's history, I just wanted to know who the fuck he was. "Name?"

Carter hesitated. "McCann. Kenneth McCann."

"Repeat that?" My body went cold as fear settled deep in my bones. McCann? No fucking way.

Carter sucked in a sharp breath. "Is that McCann as in... Brent McCann?" His voice held confusion and an edge of anger. "Who the hell is he?"

I gritted my molars so hard I feared they'd crack. "He's

Brent's father. Janine's ex-husband." *Goddamn it.* "I gotta go."

Without waiting for a response, I ended the call and clenched the phone in my hand, desperately struggling to maintain my composure. How long had Janine been working with Kenneth to jeopardize the company? And Mia. How the hell could they even think of hurting her? I knew she and Janine had never been close, but *fuck.*

The driveway markers for Bruce's—*Mia's*—cabin came into view and I slowed to a stop, parking far enough away that the Tahoe would be partially concealed by the trees. No need to draw attention to myself before it was necessary. I needed to get in there undetected so I could assess the situation and get Mia the hell away from McCann.

No fucking way was I letting the bastard get away with this.

THIRTEEN

Mia

I knelt by Bella, my hands soaked with her blood. My shoulders shook and tears streamed down my face as I tried to staunch the flow of thick red liquid oozing from the wound just over the dog's shoulder. Bella's breathing was labored, those soulful brown eyes staring up at me imploringly, as if she knew she wasn't going to make it.

A sob bubbled up my throat, fueled by anger and heartache. Behind me, I was dimly aware of footsteps moving closer.

"Get up."

I shook my head. I couldn't leave Bella here to die by herself. The German shepherd had stuck by my side for the past week while I'd healed—I wouldn't leave her now.

"Get. Up."

Cold metal pressed against the back of my head, and I immediately froze. I'd never had a gun pointed at me before, but I instinctively knew that's what I felt. My body acted out of instinct, my hands lifting as I sat back on my heels. Slowly, I climbed to my feet and turned to face him.

The gun was even scarier up close. He'd backed up a few feet, but my heart raced as I stared down the black barrel, terrified to look at it but even more afraid to take my eyes off it. At this range, he'd kill me for sure. I was cornered.

Think, Mia, think.

Everything I'd ever read said to make a run for it, try to fight back. But when it truly came down to it, I froze, unable to do anything. My lungs threatened to cause me to hyperventilate, shallow breaths making my chest rise and fall erratically. I barely refrained from darting a glance at the front door. Even if I tried to run, there was no way I could escape before he got off a shot. I could break for the kitchen and grab a knife, but it would be no match for the deadly pistol he held trained on me. I'd be dead before I could blink.

"Move." He tipped his chin toward the front door.

"Where are we going?" Hope flared in my chest. If he wanted me dead, wouldn't he just do it right here? He'd already hurt Bella. What would stop him from doing the same thing to me?

"Outside."

"Why?" I inched my way across the room, my gaze still trained on the gun in my face. My feet felt heavy and uncoordinated as they carried me backward.

"Don't want to kill you in here." His mouth twisted into a sneer of disdain. "Got enough of a mess as it is."

My heart dropped to my toes, and any hope I'd harbored fled. Still, if I could make it outside, I could try to make a break for it.

Focused on orchestrating my escape, I wasn't paying

attention and tripped over the edge of the rug. As I tried to regain my balance, my socks slid on the hardwood floor and I fell clumsily to my hands and knees.

"Goddammit!"

The barrel of the pistol connected with my face as he backhanded me, and I sucked in a sharp breath as pain exploded across my cheek. I blinked rapidly, trying to dispel the tears that had popped into my eyes.

"Get your ass moving." Kenneth stared down at me with cold, hard eyes.

I stumbled to my feet, hands held up in front of me placatingly. It was only a few feet to the front door now. I began to edge that way, feeling for the wood of the door. He must have anticipated my actions, though, because he was beside me in an instant.

The gun pressed into my side as he grasped a handful of hair in one hand and yanked roughly. "If you so much as scream, I'll shoot you where you stand. Understood?"

Clenching my eyes closed against the pain tearing across my scalp, I tried to nod. "Y-yes."

"Don't make a sound."

With one last tug to my hair, he loosened his hold and turned the knob. Inching the door open, he peeked outside before pushing it wide. "Outside."

The biting sting of the wind cut into my flesh as he guided us down the steps into the snow. I gasped as my feet sank into the powder, so cold it felt as if it were burning my flesh. The socks I wore offered no protection from the elements, the chill immediately penetrating the thin material.

I pushed on as he led us through the copse of trees out back and into a small clearing. I recognized it from yesterday when Bella had treed the chattering squirrel.

God, that seemed like a lifetime ago now. I paused, a shiver wracking my body as the wind cut through the trees, making the bare branches dance and sway. Kenneth shoved me roughly from behind, and I sank to the ground as my legs gave out, my muscles quivering with exhaustion.

I froze on my hands and knees, then lifted my head to gaze at him. I couldn't go on like this; every inch of me ached, the chill seeping into my bones. If I was going to die cold and alone, I at least needed to know the truth. "Why are you doing this?"

"You know why."

No, I really didn't. I didn't know how anyone could be so evil. My scathing glare didn't diminish his derisive smirk.

"As soon as Janine told me your father was sick, I knew it was finally my chance." He stared down at me, his head tipped slightly to one side. "I've been working here for two years. Did you know that?" I shook my head, and he continued. "No one would hire me after I came home."

Suddenly, my mind made the connection: why he looked so familiar, how I knew him. He was Brent's father. They had the same features, only Kenneth had been aged by time and stress. I knew he'd been to prison, but I couldn't remember what he'd been found guilty of. Tax evasion? Some kind of fraud? Whatever it was, he hadn't served nearly enough time.

"I had to come crawling to your father. The bastard made me start from the ground up." His handsome mouth twisted into a sneer. "God, I hated him so much. I thought once I'd taken care of him that it was all over. But no. Then you had to come along and fuck everything up. I should have been able to skim some money off the top for the next couple years until I was ready to leave. But as soon as you showed up, started talking with the crew, telling everyone you were stepping into your father's shoes, I knew I had to get rid of you. I couldn't risk anyone taking a closer look and figuring it out."

I wisely kept my mouth shut that Jack knew someone was embezzling money. Kenneth would slowly hang himself, I was sure of it. He was too confident; his arrogance would be his downfall.

I stared at him. "So it's been you this whole time."

"Of course. Want to know a little secret?"

Not really. I nodded anyway.

"I was the last person to see your father alive."

My brows drew together. That didn't make sense. "But he was..." I shook my head. "Wait."

Kenneth nodded, a malicious grin spreading over his face. "It was easy enough. I just waited until he was asleep, then placed a pillow over his face and waited."

Oh, God. The thought made me want to throw up.

"He gave you a chance, and this is how you repay him?" Fury turned the edges of my vision black as I spat the words. "And for what? Money?"

He shrugged unrepentantly. "Money makes the world go round, doll face."

My body flushed hot with rage as I glared into his eyes —eyes that my father had seen just before his death. "I hate you."

My eyes burned with anger and unshed tears, but Kenneth only laughed. "Hate me all you want, love. Won't change a thing. I'm going to kill you and dump your body in the woods where no one will ever find you."

"You think so?" I shot back. "People are up here all the time."

"Really? You're smarter than that." His lips quirked in condescension. "The animals will get to you before anyone even knows you're missing. By the time spring comes and the snow melts, you'll be long gone, scattered all over this mountain."

My mouth went dry. No one was coming for me. Brent had no idea that I was in trouble, and Jack... I prayed to God he wouldn't mourn me too much. We'd shared incredibly tender moments together this past week and a half. I wanted a lifetime more of it, but at least I would die knowing that, for a brief moment in time, he'd loved me again.

I glared up at him defiantly. "Jack will kill you."

A smirk tipped the corner of his mouth. "He can try, but he won't live long enough."

My heart pounded at the thought. Jack was an innocent in all of this. They could have my share of the company as long as they left Jack alone. "You wouldn't."

He lifted a brow. "No one will think twice when he dies of an apparent gunshot to the head, since his wife just ran off. Again."

FOURTEEN

Jack

Slipping through the trees, I made my way down the hill to the back of the house. The door was locked, and I silently sent up a prayer of thanks that I'd had copies of Bruce's keys made. I pulled the ring from my pocket, then slipped the key into the lock. The knob turned with ease, and I pushed against the door, praying it wouldn't alert anyone to my presence. It opened a fraction of an inch, then stopped as it met resistance. I shoved a bit harder and heard a thump as whatever had been stacked in front of the door hit the ground. I froze, listening intently, but the house remained quiet. I slipped through the space, then closed the door behind me.

Keeping to the wall, I made my way out of the laundry room and into the hallway. My throat constricted and my heart faltered when I spotted her. Bella was lying on the floor, a pool of dark blood surrounding her. The pantry door to my right was a splintered mess, and I could only guess what had happened here. For a brief second I closed my eyes and fury welled up within me, stirring my anger and vengeance.

Tears stinging my eyes, I knelt beside the dog and placed a gentle hand on her side. I was shocked and relieved to feel her chest rise and fall. I prayed we could get her help before it was too late. But first, I had to find Mia.

I didn't dare speak as I petted Bella once more, knowing it might be the last. Pushing to my feet, I peeked around the corner into the great room. It was quiet—too fucking quiet. Other than the soft breaths panting from Bella's mouth, I didn't hear a thing.

They should be here. Where the hell were they? Overwhelming sadness gripped me, cracking my chest wide open. Fuck. Was I too late?

With more than a little trepidation, I circled the kitchen counter, relieved that nothing greeted me on the other side. On silent feet, I was cutting across the living room toward the staircase when a slight movement outside caught my eye. I paused, deathly still, scanning for whatever had grabbed my attention.

There.

My eyes narrowed as the plush needles of the pine bough bobbed once more before returning to its resting place. It was too high up for an animal. Which meant only one thing... they were headed into the woods. Silently, I made my way outside and began to track.

Snow crunched lightly under my boots as I crept through the woods. The low tenor of voices floated on the cool breeze, and I followed them like a beacon. Sticking carefully to the existing tracks, I kept to the cover of the trees as much as possible so I wouldn't give away my position.

The voices grew louder, and I could see the outline of two figures about fifteen yards ahead. My heart jumped to my throat as the man shoved Mia to the ground and pointed a pistol at her. I wanted to lunge at him, but I was still too far away. Moving as quickly as I could without making noise, I skirted the clearing and approached him from behind.

Kenneth's words cut through the quiet air, stopping me in my tracks. "I was the last person to see your father alive."

My mind spun at the implication. The day before Bruce passed away, I had spent hours at the facility with him. He'd been there for a little over a week at that point, but I'd made sure to stop by every day or so. I'd already lost Mia, and without Bruce, I had nothing, no one close to me. So I'd gone there every day to sit with him and talk. I pretended to ask questions about the business, but we both knew the situation for what it was. Our time together was coming to a close, but I never dreamed it would end so quickly. So what the hell did Kenneth have to do with it?

A red haze filled my vision as the truth of Bruce's last day fell from the man's lips. Fury erupted inside me. Kenneth had taken Bruce away, and now Mia's fate was in his hands. I wouldn't let Kenneth take her too.

Using every ounce of training I'd accumulated in the service, I stealthily crept forward, emotions concealed, buried deep. I couldn't afford to think about Bruce right now. I couldn't even look at Mia for fear of distraction. If I saw that look in her eyes—the fear, the pain of death—I'd lose my mind. Praying that the sheriff wasn't far behind, I moved in on Kenneth. My fingers itched, my side piece practically burning me through its holster. He deserved to die, but I couldn't do that to Mia. She'd experienced enough loss, and I refused to add weight to her conscience.

Focused completely on Kenneth, I closed the distance just as he lifted the pistol toward Mia. I knew the moment she saw me, because her eyes widened the slightest fraction. I came in low for a tackle just as Kenneth whipped toward me and pulled the trigger.

FIFTEEN

Mia

A faint movement caught my attention, momentarily dragging my gaze away from Kenneth. Over the man's shoulder, a familiar figure appeared, skulking between the trees like a specter. Familiar dark eyes were narrowed with determination, his lips set in a firm line of anger. Relief flowed through my body, immediately followed by fear. I'd put Jack in danger. If Kenneth saw him...

But I was too late. Following the direction of my gaze, Kenneth whipped around, pistol raised. Jack sprang forward at the exact same time, and a shot thundered through the silent air. For a split second, time stopped. A scream stuck in my throat, my heart thundering in my chest as the icy air constricted my lungs. We all froze as if trying to process exactly what had happened. Then all hell broke loose.

The report of the gunshot and resulting crack of splintered wood as the bullet struck a tree sent a flock of birds fleeing from the tops of the trees. The cacophony was drowned out by the confusion dulling my senses. Jack lunged toward Kenneth, grasping his forearm and shoving the gun to the side. I flinched as a second shot went off, but I couldn't move, rendered motionless with fear as I watched the man I loved fight for his life—and mine.

In front of me, both men continued to move, each grappling for control, sliding precariously in the slick snow. I heard my name, but it seemed so far away. Jack's voice finally cut through my fog of confusion.

"Mia! Go!"

I darted out of the way just as the two men crashed to the ground right where I'd been standing. I scrabbled for purchase in the snow, my feet half-frozen and refusing to cooperate. They were so cold I barely felt them now, but I couldn't bring myself to worry about it—I'd put Jack in danger, and it was my responsibility to help him. I'd seen firsthand what Kenneth was capable of. Thoughts of Bella popped into my head, the way he hadn't hesitated to aim and fire at an innocent creature. No way was I letting Jack take the man on all by himself.

I slipped and fell hard to my hands and knees. Sinking into the powdery snow, my fingertips brushed something hard and rough, and they closed around a thick branch. I jerked at the limb, but it refused to come free. I dug frantically at the snow, levering my weight against it to pull it up. With a sharp snapping sound, it released from the frozen ground and I fell to my butt.

Behind me, the muted sound of scuffling filled the air, punctuated by low grunts and coarse epithets. I threw a quick look over my shoulder, and my eyes widened in horror as Kenneth rolled and straddled Jack's torso, pinning him to the ground. Jack had one hand around Kenneth's throat, and Kenneth's face was red from exhaustion and lack of oxygen. The pistol was still in his hand, and he raised it to Jack's face. Jack's free hand flew up, and his fingers wrapped around the wrist of the hand holding the pistol, trying to direct it away from him. Kenneth let out a sharp cry as Jack put pressure on the bones, and Kenneth's finger squeezed the trigger just as Jack pushed up. The shot went wide, and I flinched as bark splintered off the tree behind me and the shards flew through the air.

Jack used Kenneth's brief distraction to release his throat, and he managed to get one good blow to the man's face, catching him off guard.

The men rolled again, and I struggled to my feet, grasping the heavy limb. I shifted it in my hands, holding it like a bat, ready to swing the next time Kenneth came close. I watched in grim horror as they rolled and grappled, their motions a blur as each fought for control. I couldn't risk hitting Jack. Spreading my hands out for better leverage, I tightened my fingers around the branch. I had to time it just right.

I watched as Jack took control, pinning Kenneth beneath him, his hands wrapped tightly around the other man's neck. Face red, Kenneth used one hand to pry Jack's fingers loose. I drew in a sharp breath as the dark barrel of the gun flashed in the light, coming even with Jack's face once more. Not wasting a second, I swung as hard as I could. The branch connected with Kenneth's forearm, eliciting a cry of surprise and pain from the man. The firearm flew from his grasp and disappeared beneath the heavy layer of snow.

Jack used the opportunity to grab Kenneth's arm and wrench it behind him, at the same time rolling him to his stomach. Jack pinned him facedown, weight settled heavily on Kenneth's legs to keep him immobile. He yanked

Kenneth's arms behind his back, and the man let out a shriek of agony. Another inch and they would pop out of the sockets. "Don't fucking move!"

I flinched at the sight and turned away, tuning out the low thrum of conversation as Kenneth hurled insults at Jack. Adrenaline had kicked in, but was now starting to quickly fade away, and I was brutally aware of the biting, freezing cold. The branch fell from my useless hands, landing at my feet. My fingers ached, but my toes were now completely numb. With a small whimper, I leaned against the tree trunk and closed my eyes, willing the pain to go away.

"Mia?"

Jack's deep voice floated toward me, and I cracked my eyes open to meet his concerned gaze. "You hanging in there?"

All I could manage was a curt nod, too cold and scared and exhausted to offer anything more. His intense gaze didn't waver as he studied me, and I stared right back. There were so many things on the tip of my tongue, but I couldn't bring myself to speak.

A black blur cut through the air, and Kenneth's elbow clipped Jack's nose, taking advantage of the distraction.

"Son of a bitch!" Blood spurted from his nose, trickling over his lips and dripping from his chin.

Kenneth shoved Jack to the side, landing a volley of punches in his face. He was on his feet and advancing toward me before I had the chance to scream. Raising my hands in a defensive stance, I prepared to fend him off. I grasped Kenneth's forearm as one hand wrapped around my throat, the other looping around my middle and whipping us around. Placing me in the middle, Kenneth used me as a shield between himself and Jack.

From the corner of my eyes, I saw the steam rise from Kenneth's mouth as he spoke. "On your knees, Prescott."

Eyes filled with fury, Jack took a step backward, then dropped first to one knee, then the other. My heart raced, and Kenneth's fingers tightened where they circled my neck. "Don't try anything stupid."

His hand moved from my neck up into my hair, and I let out a sharp cry as he yanked hard, pulling me with him. Skirting Jack, Kenneth moved us in a wide arc, sweeping his foot through the soft powder. Jack's gaze met mine and never wavered. With me between them, Jack couldn't do anything—he wouldn't risk hurting me. I needed to find a way to distract Kenneth, to get him to let go of me. Before I could come up with anything, I saw the black outline in the snow, and my heart dropped to my toes.

"Ah." Kenneth picked up the pistol and wiped it on his pantleg to clear the snow stuck to the handle before raising it to the side of my face.

The cold barrel brushed my temple as I shook my head. "Please—"

The cold made it hard to think, to breathe, and I thought I was hallucinating as I glanced across the clearing and saw a shadow move between the trees. Caught between the irrational urge to laugh and cry, I sobbed out an inhuman sound as I swayed on my feet. Sheriff Donahue appeared, gun raised, splintering Kenneth's attention. In the blink of an eye, I watched Jack reach behind him just as Kenneth swung the gun toward Eric. My vision began to fade, and two gunshots pierced the air just as my legs gave out.

SIXTEEN

Jack

A profound fury engulfed me and exploded outward as I watched him press the gun to her head. Mia's gaze darted over my shoulder and widened. Barely a second later, Kenneth swung the firearm away from her, redirecting it across the clearing. His face registered surprise, and he stumbled slightly as her body swayed against him then crumpled to the ground.

In the space of two heartbeats, my Kimber was in hand and sighted on Kenneth. With a calm exhale, I squeezed the trigger. A second shot pierced the air as I felt the Kimber kick back in my hand. Donahue's shot pierced the man's midsection, ripping through the thick green fabric of his coat. Where the sheriff had been shooting to wound, I hadn't been so kind. A tiny trickle of blood seeped from the wound I'd left in his forehead as he pitched forward, collapsing partially on top of Mia.

I shoved the pistol in my waistband and scrambled toward her, shoving Kenneth's body to the side. Scooping my free hand beneath her legs, I cradled her in my arms as an unnatural red hue saturated the snow. I stood, holding her securely to my chest. Her head fell heavily against my shoulder, and I knew she was borderline hypothermic. For the first time, I noticed that her feet were covered only with a thin pair of socks. The sight of them, now soaked through, made me want to kill that asshole all over again.

A familiar voice drew my attention as Eric appeared at my shoulder, two deputies flanking him. "Nice shot."

His tone was dry, but I wasn't in the mood for his shit. Hugging Mia closer, I leveled him with a look. "She's fucking freezing; I've gotta get her inside."

His eyes darted between the limp woman in my arms and the dead man at my feet. One brow lifted in question. "She okay?"

No. "Yeah." I hoped.

One hand moved to the radio at his shoulder, his shrewd gaze not missing a single detail as it swept over us. "You need EMS?"

"I'll let you know." His chin dipped in a curt nod, and I took several steps before halting in my tracks. I shot a look over my shoulder. "Sheriff?"

He lifted an inquisitive brow.

"Bella's in the kitchen." My chest rose on a ragged breath. "I don't know if she's..."

His face hardened, and I thought I saw a trace of pity in his hazel gaze. "I'll take care of it."

Trusting him to do as he promised, I strode through the trees, using my shoulders to block the branches from hitting Mia where she rested against my chest. Blood dripped from my nose onto her sweater, and the sight pissed me off all over again. I couldn't believe I'd let that slippery fucker get the drop on me while my attention had been on Mia. I lifted my shoulder and used my shirt to brush away the sticky fluid.

Less than a minute later, I vaulted up the porch steps and pushed through the front door. My woman was safe in my arms, but I knew Bella was still in here. I swallowed hard as I kicked the door shut behind us. I couldn't bring myself to glance in that direction. I knew if I did, I'd lose my shit. I'd had to make a split-second decision—one I wouldn't take back even if I could. Mia would be dead now if I hadn't gone after her.

Anger took over, and I carried Mia up to the master bedroom, channeling all my energy into getting her warm. Inside the bathroom, I held her close as I flipped the handle to turn on the shower. She shivered in my arms, her tremors vibrating against my skin. I wanted to get her out of those cold, wet clothes and under the warm water. Cautiously, I set her on her feet, but she swayed unsteadily. I tightened my hold and lowered her to the edge of the tub.

"Sit here for just a second, sweetheart."

Another set of shivers wracked her body, and her hands curled around the lip of the tub, knuckles white with strain as she fought to keep herself upright. I quickly shrugged out of my coat, then shed my shirt and jeans, one hand on Mia's shoulder to keep her from tipping over. As soon as I was down to my underwear, I scooped her up and stepped into the shower with her still in my arms. The water wasn't even lukewarm yet but the heat stung our frozen skin, and Mia let out a miserable groan.

"Shh, baby. I know." I nuzzled her hair. "Gotta get you warmed up."

Sinking to my knees, I cradled her close and settled her across my lap, angling her so my body would take the brunt of the direct spray. Reaching over, I plugged the drain, and the tub gradually began to fill. Pulling off her socks, I examined her tiny feet, the flesh already turning a deep purple from the cold. Dipping her feet into the water so they would begin to thaw, I massaged the flesh to stimulate the blood flow. As her body warmed and the shivers began to subside, I increased the temperature of the water. When the tub had filled almost to the top, I turned off the shower and sank into the warm liquid.

I rested her head against my chest and stroked one hand over her cool, damp hair. Most of a person's heat was lost through the scalp's surface, and I knew I had to get her head under the water. "Lean back, sweetheart."

Mia shook her head, her arms tightening around my neck. "N-no. C-can't."

"Yes, you can. Come on," I urged. I gently peeled her arms away and supported her shoulders as I tipped her back. "You got this."

Tears leaked from the corners of her eyes, and I couldn't watch any longer. I lifted her up and pressed her face to my chest again, holding her close. "Okay, baby. It's okay."

Her body trembled violently. "Bella?"

I swallowed hard. "I don't know."

Her forehead dropped to my chest, and her shoulders shook. I held her as she cried, tears stinging the backs of my eyelids. I was fucking torn. I wanted to go check, but I couldn't let go of the woman in my arms. How the fuck was I going to choose?

We sat there in silence, both of us grieving everything we'd lost. When her tears began to subside, I coasted one hand down her back. "How are you feeling?"

"Better." She sat up but avoided my gaze, and I watched as a stray tear slid down her cheek.

Automatically, my hand lifted to brush it away, but I

curled it into a fist and dropped it to my lap. There was so much between us now, and I wouldn't push her. I wanted to touch her—I wanted to never let go of her again—but she had to make the decision to meet me halfway.

Mia cleared her throat and lifted one arm, watching as water cascaded from the fabric of her shirt sleeve. "We should go get dressed."

"Stay here." I shifted her off of me and stood, water sluicing off my body. Mia turned her head slightly away, but I could feel her gaze on me as I stepped from the tub. Peeling off my sodden socks and underwear, I tossed them in the sink to drain, then grabbed a towel from the rack and wrapped it around my waist.

Scooping up my clothes, I carried them into the bedroom and quickly redressed, opting to go commando instead of digging around to find anything Bruce had left behind. Mia's clothes were still in the plastic shopping bags, and I pulled out a pair of yoga pants and a warm sweater. Touching her lingerie felt wrong, so I quickly dug out a pair of panties and a bra, then carried everything back to the bathroom.

"Here." I set the pile of clothes on the vanity. "Take your time."

Without waiting for a response, I closed the door behind me and headed out of the bedroom. I steeled myself as I descended the stairs to the great room, my gaze drawn to the hallway. Eric knelt beside Bella, one hand stroking over her fur.

His gaze jumped to mine and he tipped his chin. "Breathing is shallow but she's here."

I let out a relieved breath and grabbed a blanket from the couch as I passed. "We need to get her to the truck."

I dropped to one knee beside the dog, murmuring softly

as I shook the blanket open. Eric took a corner and spread the blanket out so we could use it as a makeshift stretcher. I could pick her up and carry her to the Tahoe, but I didn't want to cause any more damage to the muscle than there already was.

I felt her before I saw her, and I turned to look at Mia. One hand covered her mouth, agony in her eyes as she stared at Bella, and I couldn't help reaching out and taking her hand. "She's hanging in there, but we need to get her some help."

Mia dropped to her knees and laid her face on the floor next to Bella's. The sight damn near broke me. I tore my gaze away and jerked my chin at Eric. "Help me."

SEVENTEEN

Mia

Heart wrenching with pain and regret, I gazed into Bella's soulful dark eyes. God, this was all my fault. I never should have let him in. I'd done this to her. "I'm so sorry, girl."

My voice broke as tears coasted down my cheeks. The scene replayed itself in my mind over and over. I heard the wood crack and give way, and I saw the flash of the matte black barrel swing toward the pantry. The report of gunfire echoed in my ears and the howl of pain as Bella collapsed to the ground.

"Mia, honey." I barely acknowledged the sound of Jack's voice. "We've gotta get her up."

I scooted out of the way as Jack and Eric carefully maneuvered a blanket under Bella, who let out a miserable cry. Tears filled my eyes once again and I pressed a hand over my mouth to stem the sob bubbling up my throat.

Eric laid a hand on my shoulder. "Closest vet is in Kalispell. Grab the keys, we're going to load her up."

Relieved to have a mission, I scooped up the keys and

ran out to Jack's Tahoe to open the back gate. The two men carried the dog out and set her in the back. I tossed the keys to Jack and hopped up inside. "I'm riding with her."

I wanted to make sure she was comfortable, but I also wanted her to know she wasn't alone, in case...

I threw a look at Jack. He looked absolutely devastated, and I wanted so badly to reach out and grab his hand, tell him everything was going to be okay. But I couldn't. I had no idea what the next few hours would bring.

Eric slammed the gate, and twenty seconds later we were churning out of the driveway and down the mountain. The drive was silent except for the hum of the wheels against the pavement and Bella's stilted breathing. I stroked her head, careful not to stray too low and touch the wound.

The trip seemed interminable as Jack sped through Pine Ridge and continued down to Kalispell. The longest hour of my life passed in a blur of gray skies and tall pines through the back window as Bella labored to breathe beside me.

I heard Jack on the phone with the veterinarian's office, letting them know we were on the way, and ten minutes later the Tahoe came to a halt. My heart jumped in my chest as Jack opened the back gate. I slid out just as a woman in a white lab coat came around the vehicle with an assistant in tow. I stood back as they carried Bella inside and back to an exam room.

Jack propped his hands on his hips and paced nervously. The woman at the desk offered a sympathetic smile and handed me a clipboard with paperwork. I glanced at Jack, then began to fill out what I could. The strain around his eyes was showing, and he prowled the small waiting area like a panther.

After I'd filled out what I could, I carried the paperwork

back to the receptionist. "I'll have him fill out the rest later," I said quietly.

She nodded as if she understood. "That's fine."

I sank into a chair and pulled my feet up, tucking my chin against my knees. I closed my eyes and listened as Jack stalked restlessly about the room. The ordeal with Kenneth was over, but I wasn't sure we'd ever overcome the destruction he'd left in his wake.

EIGHTEEN

Jack

Three fucking hours.

The second hand on the clock made another taunting circle, bleeding into another minute that we'd been waiting in agonizing worry. I raked one hand through my hair and closed my eyes. The events of the morning played on a loop in my mind over and over. A thousand times I watched Mia fall to her knees in the snow, staring up at Kenneth with a combination of fear and bravery.

I shot a quick glance across the room. She sat in the corner with her legs pulled up, her chin resting on her knees. She looked vulnerable and frail, and I wanted more than anything to go to her and pull her into my arms. I wanted to apologize, to tell her how much she meant to me. But I swallowed down the words.

I sank into a chair and cradled my head in my hands. What the fuck was I going to do? I'd lost Mia, and now I was losing Bella, too. It was too fucking much to deal with.

Popping out of the chair, I stormed across the room to the small reception desk. "Any idea how much longer?"

"I'm sorry, sir." She shook her head. "We'll let you know as soon as the doctor is done."

Heaving a sigh, I crossed back to my seat. I could feel Mia's eyes on me the whole way, but I refused to make contact. I couldn't. If I saw that look in her eyes, it'd fucking gut me. The room was silent except for the shuffling of papers and tapping of keys as the receptionist entered information into the computer.

Standing, I approached her once more. "Miss?"

"Yes?" She tipped her head.

Fuck. I needed something to do, something to keep my hands busy and my mind off Bella. "Do you need me to fill anything out?"

"Let me double check." She reached for a clipboard. "We only need the payment information. Your wife filled out everything else."

My heart constricted at the term as I took the paperwork. "Thank you."

My gaze flitted over the form, Mia's pretty handwriting filling the blanks. Just below my name, the address listed stopped me cold. She'd listed our old address. My mind spun. Had she used it out of habit? I still had no idea exactly how much she remembered, but she seemed to have recalled our fight that last day. So why would she list our old house on there?

I still owned it, but she didn't know that. Did she? I shoved the thought from my mind. It didn't matter—not really. Except I couldn't shake the feeling that for some reason, it meant everything. I flicked a glance over my shoulder. She remained huddled in the corner, back to the wall as she held onto her legs for dear life, as though if she let go she might float away.

It killed me to see her like that, so unsure of herself. I couldn't imagine what was going through her mind right now. She'd watched as Bella had been shot and was held at gunpoint herself by some selfish fuck who wanted her money—an asshole who'd died at my hands. I'd never wanted her to see that side of me, but I'd do it a thousand times over if it meant keeping her safe.

She hadn't looked me in the eyes since she watched Kenneth's lifeless body crumple to the ground. It made me want to kill him all over again.

A door to my right opened and the veterinary assistant stepped out. "Mr. and Mrs. Prescott?"

I tipped my chin but didn't correct her. "That's us."

"Come with me, please."

Dread congealed in my gut. I didn't want to acknowledge what could be waiting in the exam room. Her expression and tone gave nothing away, and I steeled myself as Mia came to my side. Outwardly, I pasted on a calm façade but inside I was losing it. It felt like everything was slipping through my fingers like grains of sand through an hourglass. It was falling apart so quickly I couldn't catch it and put it back together.

Mia's shoulder brushed mine, sending my pulse skittering through my veins. Silently we followed the young woman to an exam room at the end of the hallway. The veterinarian stood by the steel table where Bella lay still—so still. I paused in the doorway, almost unable to continue on. A tiny hand slipped into mine, and I squeezed Mia's fingers so hard I was sure I'd hurt her. Swallowing hard, I loosened my hold and stepped into the room with Mia by my side.

Somehow we'd get through this—whatever happened, I was reassured for the moment that she was still here with me.

Bags hung under the doctor's tired eyes, but she offered us a small smile nonetheless. "There was a lot of injury to the surrounding tissue, but she's stable."

I let out a sigh of relief, and Mia's hand flew to her mouth to stifle a sob. Releasing her hand, I slipped my arm around her shoulders and pulled her close. She tucked her head against my chest, and we stood there for several minutes, silently offering the other comfort.

The vet continued softly, "It'll be a long road but, barring any unforeseen complications, I expect her to make a full recovery." I nodded but couldn't speak over the lump in my throat. "I'd like to keep her at least overnight and reevaluate her in the morning."

"Of course." I cleared my throat. "Is she...?"

The vet shook her head. "It'll take a while for the meds to wear off, but you're more than welcome to stop by first thing in the morning. We'll keep her in the specialized recovery kennels out back."

Mia wiped her eyes and took a tiny step away but didn't leave my side. The next few minutes passed in a blur as we settled up the payment and got into the car. On autopilot, I drove to the closest hotel and we ventured into the packed lobby. I glanced at the man behind the registration desk. "We'd like two rooms, please."

The elderly clerk's eyes skimmed over us as he took in our messy, bloodstained clothes. It pissed me off, but I understood his wariness, so I decided to let him off the hook. "We'll only need a night or two. We just left the emergency vet clinic over on Broad Street."

The man tipped his head in understanding, a combination of relief and pity filling his eyes. "Ah. Let me see what I can find for you."

His fingers flew over the keyboard for only a moment before he paused and met my gaze. I hadn't asked Mia how she felt about it, but I assumed she'd want her space. I should've known by the number of people milling around outside that it wasn't going to happen.

The elderly man grimaced. "I'm sorry, sir. We only have one room available, but it's a queen. The park is only a block away, so you'll be close to the festivities."

I blinked. "I'm sorry, we're not from around here. What's going on?"

"Oh." The man laughed. "This is Winterfest."

I didn't know what the hell that meant, but it was obviously a big deal.

"Lodging is pretty scarce right now," he warned. "Winterfest brings people from all over the tri-state area."

He slid a flier across the counter and continued with a rundown of the week-long itinerary. I didn't give a shit about festivities. The last thing I wanted to do was pretend to be happy. I scrubbed a palm over my face. "That sounds wonderful. We'll take it."

Tossing my credit card on the counter, I debated what the hell I was going to do—with life, with the woman standing stiff as a board beside me. *Fuck.* It was going to be a long damn night.

NINETEEN

Mia

My heart hurt. For Bella, for Jack... but also for me. What little hope I'd harbored fled the moment I heard Jack ask for two rooms. I shouldn't be surprised. Once again, I'd cast him aside without listening to him, without trusting him. He had no reason to want me. Hell, I couldn't even stand me right now. I'd been awful to him.

I studied Jack surreptitiously out of the corner of my eyes. He looked haggard and angry all at once. I didn't know what to say, so I just pressed my lips into a tight line.

With a resigned sigh, Jack swept a hand over his face. "We'll take it."

My heart plummeted at his tone, and I dropped my gaze away, pretending to study the people filling the streets. I knew nothing of Kalispell, but it seemed that what the clerk said was true: there must be thousands of people outside. I hadn't noticed on our way in, my mind on the events of the morning, but people carried food from various vendors' booths, checking out artwork and holding ice skates. I wondered if there was a pond or outdoor rink nearby for people to skate on, like in Rockefeller Center. The thought made me smile.

The clerk swiped the credit card that Jack tossed on the counter, and we made our way to the single elevator around the corner. While we waited for the lift to arrive, I studied my reflection in the steel. Bella's blood streaked across my shirt and pants from where I'd knelt beside her. Jack seemed to know exactly what I was thinking, because only a second later, his voice came out low and soft. "I'll see if any shops in town deliver."

I bobbed my head, swallowing down the lump in my throat. "Thanks."

The elevator dinged, and the doors slid open with a whoosh. Silently, we stepped inside, and Jack stabbed the button for the sixth floor. He leaned against the wall in a pose of relaxation with his hands shoved in his pockets, but I knew it was a ruse. I took in the stiff set to his shoulders, the firm line of his jaw. He was angry—but at whom?

I didn't have time to ponder, let alone ask the question. The doors slid open, depositing us on the sixth floor. Jack pushed off the wall and strode out of the car without a second glance, and I followed quietly behind. Halfway down the hallway, he inserted the card into the door on the right, and it beeped as it unlocked. Holding the door open with one arm, Jack stood to the side and allowed me to pass him. Once we were both inside, he threw the lock and deadbolt.

We stared at each other for several long moments before Jack finally broke the silence. "Would you like to shower?"

I glanced down at my clothes again and grimaced. I was still cold all over, like my body was still half-frozen, and I felt unclean, as if today's events had somehow tainted me. I wanted to wash away the sensation of filthiness that Kenneth's touch had left on my skin.

Swallowing hard, I met his gaze. "Yeah, if you don't mind."

"No problem." He lumbered toward the desk in the corner. "I'll be right here."

With a quick nod, I stepped into the bathroom and closed the door behind me. Almost desperately, I peeled out of my clothes and stepped under the hot spray. Too many bad things had happened, and I wanted to rinse it all away. I scrubbed at my skin with the hotel-issue soap until I turned pink, and I let it all run down the drain.

Tears mingled with water and dripped down my face. Since we'd left the veterinarian's office, it was like Jack had flipped a switch. He didn't look at me unless he had to, and he didn't touch me. I wish I knew what he was thinking. Unfortunately, I had a feeling I already knew. I'd pushed him away, so he was shutting down to protect himself.

Determination steeled my spine. It wasn't the ideal time, but I needed to talk to him, and this might be my only opportunity. Somehow I had to get him to listen so I could tell him how I really felt. If he turned me away...

I swallowed hard. This time around I was going to do what was best for Jack. And if that meant walking away forever—even at the risk of sacrificing my heart—I would do it. Because he deserved it.

TWENTY

Jack

I heard the water turn on in the bathroom, and I ran a hand through my hair as I sank into the chair. Closing my eyes, I allowed my head to drop back as I slouched dejectedly. I had no fucking idea what to do next. If I thought things had been bad before, they couldn't compare to the shit we'd been through in the past eight hours.

Before the ordeal with Kenneth and Bella, I swore Mia had been about to breach the gap between us. But seeing her now, aqua eyes sad and aloof, walls back up, I knew I must have been wrong. And I couldn't even blame her. Kenneth was retaliating against Bruce and me, but Mia got caught in the middle by her father's scheme. It killed me that she'd been hurt—that both of my girls had been hurt—because of me. Kenneth was dead, but there were so many unanswered questions.

Digging my phone from my pocket, I pulled up the search engine to find local stores and boutiques that might deliver clothes. Both of us would need something to get us through the next day until we could get back to Briarleigh. Three calls later, I finally managed to find a store that carried both men's and women's clothing that would be willing to deliver to the hotel. It was athletic wear, but I didn't figure Mia would care. She'd never been into designer clothes and frilly baubles anyway, despite the fact that she could afford to buy whatever she wanted.

I hung up after thanks and the promise to leave a hefty tip for a quick delivery. The search for clothing had momentarily distracted me from the events that had unfolded this morning, but I could no longer put it off. I tapped the sheriff's number and waited for the call to connect.

True to form, Eric skipped the niceties and dived right in. "How is she?"

A tiny smirk lifted my mouth. "Which one?" Silence filled the line, and I sighed. "They're both okay... for now." I waited a beat when I heard a relieved breath filter through the receiver. "Bella's stable, and she's spending the next couple days recovering at the emergency vet's office here."

"And Mia?"

Genuine concern tinged his voice, and jealousy surged through me at the question. Was Eric interested in her? But as I caught my reflection in the window, a scowl decorating my face, I knew he wasn't. The sheriff had seen us—both of us—at our worst. He was genuinely concerned for her. "She's..."

I had no idea what to say, because I hadn't asked. I didn't know if she was relieved or upset that Kenneth was dead. He'd hurt Bella and tried to kill Mia, but the man had been Brent's father. I knew she'd never wish that kind of hurt on anyone, let alone someone she loved like her stepbrother. She'd experienced the pain of loss recently, and I had a feeling it would gut her. Despite the brave façade she showed the world, I knew she was sensitive and soft underneath.

"I'll keep you posted." She'd watched me kill the man. That was a lot to come back from. I'd seen death, and though I'd never enjoyed taking a life, I would never regret my actions today. Kenneth had threatened Mia's life. He'd deserved to die. If that sent me to prison, so be it.

I knew the question was on the tip of his tongue, so I answered Donahue's unspoken question. "We'll come up to the station tomorrow. You can do whatever you need to do." My voice was gruff, and I swallowed down my rioting emotions.

There was a long pause before, finally, "Since it was self-defense, I just need the official statements."

I blew out the breath I hadn't realized I'd been holding. Deep appreciation filled my tone when I was able to speak. "Thank you."

Eric ignored my thanks and changed the subject. "We brought Mrs. Hamilton in for questioning."

I sat up straight in my seat. "And?"

"We're taking care of it."

What the hell did that mean? "She—"

"Not now."

I snapped my mouth closed and slumped back in my seat. Eric didn't want to say anything over the phone, which I could understand. It was hard as fuck to just sit back and let it all play out, but the sheriff had never given me a reason not to trust him. I decided to go with my gut. "Fill me in later."

The sheriff snorted at my command. "Don't you have anything better to do, Prescott?"

"Not when it comes to Mia."

He let out a beleaguered sigh. "I assume you're bringing her with you tomorrow? I'll need her statement, too."

I fucking hated the idea of subjecting Mia to questioning after everything she'd been through, but it was procedure and there wasn't a damn thing I could do about it. "Yeah, fine."

"Good. Can you be here at ten?"

"How about eleven?" I countered. "The clinic opens at nine, and I want to check on Bella before we take off."

"No problem. Are you staying in Kalispell or heading back to Briarleigh?"

"I don't know," I hedged. "I'll probably be back and forth. I imagine Mia will want to get back home, so I'll probably drop her off at her place tomorrow."

A long pause ensued. "You sure?"

No, I didn't know a goddamn thing.

The running water cut off in the bathroom, and I knew Mia would be finished in just a moment. I turned my attention back to Eric. "Gotta go. See you at eleven."

I hit End and shoved the phone in my back pocket just as the bathroom door swung open, revealing Mia in a standard-issue white robe.

I stared at her, silently absorbing every detail. Her gaze swept over the room and caught on me as she paused midstep, suspended between the bathroom and the bedroom. I tried and failed to read her expression. There was so much emotion in those turquoise eyes I couldn't begin to decipher exactly what she was feeling.

I offered her a small smile and stood. "Clothes should be here in a bit. I'm going to shower, if you don't mind."

With a curt shake of her head, she sidestepped and allowed me to pass her. I left the door open an inch so I could hear her if anything happened. It wasn't likely, but after what had happened today, I wasn't taking any chances. I needed to know that she was safe, even locked in a hotel room six stories up. Old habits were hard to break, and my protective instincts were always on guard with her. She meant the world to me, and I was damned sure going to make sure she stayed safe.

Flipping the handle on the shower, I tested the water before stripping out of my dirty clothes and stepping under the warm spray. Though I'd technically been in the shower once already today, the first time had primarily been to get Mia warm again. Resting one hand against the fiberglass surround, I hung my head and allowed the water to cascade over me, running in rivulets down my face and dripping from my chin. I closed my eyes and saw red as I imagined Kenneth holding Mia captive again. I felt the recoil of the pistol in my hand as the bullet left the chamber. I couldn't take it back. And I wouldn't. The only thing that mattered was the woman in the room next door. I'd do it all over again —because I loved her. And I'd sacrifice my soul to keep her safe.

TWENTY-ONE

Mia

Standing by the window, I leaned my head against the cool glass and stared into the darkness. From a couple blocks over, the faint strains of music from the park floated on the night air and met my ears. Tiny yellow lights illuminated the people as they milled around, but I felt disconnected, like I was in an alternate reality. None of this felt real. I wanted to go to sleep and wake up in the morning only to discover that it was all a dream. My eyes focused on my reflection in the window. The woman there looked haunted, withdrawn. More so than I'd felt nearly a week ago when I'd woken with no memory. Maybe I could rewind this entire week.

Disappointment slammed into me, and I realized I didn't want to erase this past week. Had this not happened, I wouldn't have had the time with Jack. I had no idea what would have happened otherwise. Surely I'd have seen him at some point, since we were now partners. But would I have been receptive to him? Probably not. I'd missed him, but my pride had always gotten in the way of my happiness. That was true more now than ever. By not giving him a chance to explain, I may have lost him forever.

From behind me, I heard the bathroom door open. I glanced over my shoulder and froze as I took in Jack's muscular form. His chest bare, he'd wrapped a towel around his waist for modesty. I couldn't help the way my gaze dropped and took in every inch of him from his toes up to his slicked-back hair, still shining with water droplets from the shower.

He leveled me with his intense stare. "How are you feeling?"

"Fine." I paused, dredging up the courage to form the next words. "Do you really think Bella will be okay?"

He seemed to weigh his answer before speaking. "I'm sure they'll do their best."

I bit my lip and pinned my gaze to his bare chest, unable to look him in the eye. I had to know—I couldn't put it off anymore. "Can I ask you a question?"

Going completely rigid, Jack eyed me warily. "Sure."

I debated exactly what I wanted to say and went with the least inflammatory. "Are you mad at me?"

Blowing out a breath, Jack raked a hand through his hair, sending water droplets splattering onto his broad shoulders. He blinked once, long and slow, before meeting my eyes. "No, Mia. I'm not mad at you."

He hadn't moved an inch, but I was certain I could hear a trace of disappointment in his voice. I redirected my attention to the window to hide the moisture gathering in my eyes. "It shouldn't have happened. If I hadn't—"

"Mia." My name was a warning falling from his lips, but I ignored it.

"It's all my fault."

"No." He was in front of me before I'd even fully turned around, and he cupped my chin in one large palm. "None of this is your fault. McCann was determined to follow through no matter who or what was in his way. I'm just thankful you're alive."

My voice cracked on the whispered words. "Thank you."

"Welcome." His voice was gruff, his muscles tense as he released my chin and dropped his hand to his side. "Do you want to talk about it?"

I had no idea what I planned to say, but the words fell from my mouth before I could stop them. "I was so scared," I admitted. "He said he was going to check the fuel in the generator but then he started asking questions about how I liked it there. He forced his way inside, and I kept waiting for Brent, because he'd texted me, but..." I took a deep breath. "Kenneth had Brent's phone."

Jack nodded. "I was at the sheriff's office while Brent was being questioned. When you texted me, I knew something was wrong."

If only I'd answered the phone. I nodded, unsure of what to say now. Despite the fact that he stood just inches away, the chasm between us seemed to stretch infinitely. Only hours ago, he'd scooped me into his arms and held me close. Now he stood harsh and unyielding, seemingly a different person. Now that the stress of the morning had worn off, had he come to his senses?

I couldn't bear to ask—not yet. "You said something about clothes?"

"I called a boutique while you were in the shower. They should be here soon."

It wasn't lost on me that he'd done the exact same thing

a week ago. Despite the turmoil between us, Jack always took care of me. "Thank you."

His chin dipped in acknowledgment, and I searched for something else to say. "What now?"

Chocolate eyes pierced mine. "I can't answer that."

I didn't know if he was referring to Bella's situation or to ours, but I wanted to clear the air. "I owe you an apology." He opened his mouth to speak, but I held up a hand. "Not just for the other day, but... for last time, too."

Understanding lit his eyes at my mention of our last fight. His Adam's apple bobbed as he swallowed. "I only wanted what was best for you. For us."

I blinked back the tears burning my eyelids at his heart-breaking admission. "I know that now."

Looking back, it was all so clear. Jack had never wanted anyone's charity, especially not my father's. Dad had pulled him from an impossible situation, and enlisting was Jack's way of thanking him. He'd needed to stand on his own two feet and show my father that he was able to take care of himself and take care of me as well, completely on his own.

God, I'd been so stupid. How had I not seen it before?

"You remembered." It was a statement, not a question.

I nodded. "I was young and... selfish." Drawing in a deep breath, I continued, unable to meet his gaze. "I'm sorry for all the things I said. I couldn't—wouldn't—see it from your side." I'd been a spoiled kid who expected to have everything handed to me. "I thought you weren't happy. I thought you'd re-upped to get away from me. And when you didn't come after me..."

I trailed off, the tears filling my eyes finally spilling over. A gentle thumb swept over my cheekbone, brushing the moisture away.

"You'll never know how sorry I am." Jack dropped his

hand away and shook his head. "I regret it every day. But you seemed so happy. You'd moved on and made something of yourself. I couldn't bring myself to disrupt your life more than I already had."

I knew from the expression on his face that he was sincere, and my heart clenched with a mixture of longing and regret. I didn't deserve his forgiveness. He'd shown me over and over how much he cared about me, but I hadn't listened. Not eight years ago, and not last week when I'd been stranded in his cabin. "I wish you would've." I whispered the words. "I wish I'd done everything differently."

Jack nodded. "Me too."

God, we'd made so many mistakes. Was it even possible to come back from something like that? I pushed down the insecurity threatening to clog my throat. From here on out, I vowed to do what was right—for both of us. But there was still something I needed to know. I wrapped my arms around my waist. "What about... her?" *Sara.* I couldn't even bring myself to say her name aloud.

He grimaced, his expression pained. "It's not what you think." His hands scrubbed over his face, and he gestured to the bed. "Can we sit?"

With a slight inclination of my head, I followed his lead and sank to the edge of the bed. Instead of sitting beside me, Jack pulled the desk chair over and sat in front of me. Elbows braced on his knees, head down, he spoke. "What do you want to know?"

I stilled. Part of me wanted to hear everything—how they met, if they'd been in love. He took my hand and stared at me imploringly, waiting for my answer. I knew he'd tell me whatever I wanted to know. I hated that he'd been with her—been with any other woman besides me. But I had no one to blame but myself. I'd pushed him away and he'd moved on. I'd dated other men while we were divorced, so I couldn't cast stones. I swallowed hard, terrified to ask the question, petrified of the answer. "Do you love her?"

"No." His head shook emphatically. "She knows that. I'm still in love with you, and..."

He trailed off, and I contemplated his words, thinking over the past few days. The picture in his cabin spoke volumes, but it was the memory of Sara's words that came back to me. She'd known exactly who I was even before I'd introduced myself. Maybe it was a woman's intuition, but Sara had somehow been able to tell I was the woman from Jack's past, his true love.

Maybe there was hope for us after all. The only question was, what were we going to do about it?

TWENTY-TWO

Jack

It tore my heart out to tell her about Sara, but I refused to lie. I owed her the truth at least.

Her chest rose on an inhale before she spoke. "I don't blame you for that, for any of it."

I stared at her hand, so small and delicate in mine. I didn't deserve her—I never had. But God, I hoped she'd give me this chance to put the past to rest and move forward. I couldn't bear to look at her for fear of what I might see in her beautiful eyes.

I used my thumb to rub small circles on the back of her hand, my pulse thrumming erratically. Reiterating her question from earlier, I put the ball back in her court now that I'd laid my cards on the table. "What now?"

Her turbulent gaze sought mine. "What do you want?"

"You." The answer was immediate and filled with conviction. "I only want you."

She paused, seeming to consider my sincerity. "Did you mean what you said?"

"Every word." Everything I'd felt, every word that had come from my mouth, was genuine.

Ocean-colored eyes pierced mine. "Even when you said you loved me?"

I dipped my chin in the barest of nods. "Especially then."

The corner of her mouth twitched up in a mischievous smirk. "Forever?"

"For always." The tiniest smile lifted my lips. I knew it was going to be a long fucking road, but I'd do anything for this woman. "Can we start over?"

Instead of responding right away, she placed her palms on my cheeks, framing my face as she studied me long and hard. My lungs seized up as she slowly shook her head. "I don't want to start over."

I felt my heart fall from my chest and shatter on the floor in the silence that hung between us. I opened my mouth to say something—anything—but she silenced me with a finger to my lips.

"Every day without you I felt broken." I swallowed hard at her admission, my gut twisting into knots. "But I don't want to forget what happened. Yes, it hurt, but it took that pain for me to realize how much I love you." Relief and hope zinged through me as she continued. "Without it, I wouldn't appreciate what we have nearly as much. Love is messy and wonderfully, terribly imperfect, but it's beautiful. I want this time to be better. *I* want to be better."

Unable to stop myself, I grabbed her hips and pulled her forward into my lap until there was barely a whisper of air between us. Her hands slipped around the back of my neck, and I banded my arms around her tiny waist. A thousand thoughts and emotions jumbled my brain, hindering my speech. I wanted to freeze this moment in time; I just wanted to *feel*. Her soft breath against my ear. The warmth of her skin pressed to mine. The fluttering of her pulse under my lips where they rested at the base of her neck.

"You are perfect." I pulled back a fraction and dropped my forehead to hers. "Every day without you was a blur, like I was just going through the motions. But then you showed up and breathed life into me again. You gave me a reason to get up each day and go on."

Her chest brushed mine as it rose on a shuddering inhale, and her whispered words caressed my mouth. "I missed you so much. Even before I came to Briarleigh." I remembered the words she'd whispered that first night when she'd shown up, delirious and half-frozen. *Missed you.* I'd been terrified to acknowledge her admission, praying it was true. She struggled to formulate her next words. "You make me... I haven't felt whole since..."

She trailed off, flustered. I knew exactly how she felt. "Mia?"

"Yeah?" Her breath hit my lips as she spoke.

"I'm gonna kiss you."

I waited a single heartbeat to make sure she wasn't going to refuse. Turned out, I didn't have to wait. Her face tipped upward, her mouth already seeking mine. I sucked her bottom lip into my mouth, my tongue darting out to taste her. A low groan bubbled up my throat. Goddamn, it'd been too long. Rationally, I knew it'd only been a few days, but still... Even a few hours without her was too much.

Between her widespread legs, my cock jumped to attention, eager to be free of the towel confining it. Lips never leaving hers, I pulled the sash of the robe free and slipped my hands inside to span her tiny waist, so small my fingers almost met in the middle.

She shifted in my lap as if trying to get closer, and I

lifted her, at the same time pulling her pelvis against my groin. Sealed together from hip to chest, Mia and I—we just fit. The warm skin of her stomach burned mine, and I brushed my thumbs along the sides of her breasts.

I wanted to thrust up into her, fuck her until she begged for mercy—but I needed to know that she wanted this too. Damn it. I really hated being a gentleman sometimes. Breaking the kiss, I pulled back and stared into her eyes. Even as my dick screamed at me to keep going, I asked the question. "Are you sure?"

Instead of answering, her fingers sifted through the short strands of hair at the base of my neck and pulled my head down to hers. Warm lips still damp from our kiss captured mine once more.

Good enough. Bracing one hand around her back, I tipped her slightly away from me and used my free hand to untie the towel binding my hips. My cock sprang up between us, hard and ready as it brushed the inside of her thighs. I could feel the heat from her drawing me in, and I'd been rock-hard since the moment I saw her standing by the window.

Sliding my hands beneath her butt, I lifted her over my engorged shaft. The crown prodded her opening and slipped inside, immediately enveloped by her moist heat. A groan rose into the air, and for the life of me, I didn't know if it came from her or me. She slid the whole way down until my dick was seated firmly inside her. I could feel her walls constricting around me as I filled up every inch of her, possessing her.

I lifted her up and pumped into her as I pulled her down again, setting a slow rhythm. Mia ground her hips against mine each time her clit brushed my pelvis, and her head fell back on a moan. I braced my feet against the floor and undulated my hips, thrusting as deeply into her as I could.

Fuck. It was too soon, but I couldn't hold it in any longer. I slowed my pace and looked deeply into her eyes. "I love you, Mia."

Tears filled her eyes, and a split second later her mouth crashed against mine, hungry, needy. Her tongue swept between my lips, mimicking my movements between her legs. I thrust hard and deep, feeling the first tremors wrack her body. It started slow, and the shudder gradually radiated outward as she shattered in my arms.

I tightened my hold as she let go, ready to catch her when she fell.

TWENTY-THREE

Mia

Like a match being struck, I burst into flame, my body burning and writhing as hot waves of ecstasy curled through me. Air left my lungs, my body floating, my mind blank as I succumbed to the bliss Jack pulled from me. It was better than anything I'd ever felt—better than the first time we'd made love a decade ago. Better even than our lovemaking a week ago. It was as if each time was more pleasurable than the last, the emotion carrying us away to a place where only we existed.

Beneath me, Jack continued to thrust upward, claiming my body. His fingers curled into my hips as his pace quickened, the sensation drawing out my orgasm. I ground against him, my toes scrabbling for purchase against the thin carpet. Suspended over his muscular thighs, I could barely touch the ground, and it severely limited my range of movement. From the expression on his face, I thought Jack rather liked that fact.

He felt huge from this angle, seated fully inside me,

filling up every inch. He lowered me up and down, each time hitting my G-spot and stoking the inferno building deep inside. My ragged moan filled the air as my core ignited and a second orgasm swept through me like wildfire. Jack thrust twice more and slipped one arm around my waist like a steel band, holding me in place as his warm seed flooded my pussy.

I rested my forehead on his shoulder, our chests rising and falling in the same rapid tempo. Feeling slowly returned to my limbs as I came down from my high, and I let out a soft exhalation of contentment as my skin tingled with desire.

Then, with seemingly no effort at all, Jack slid one hand under my bottom and stood with me wrapped in his arms. The weight of my body pulled me downward, and motion caused his dick to slide even deeper inside me—if that were even possible. I let out a moan and wrapped my legs around his waist to hold him there, the stimulation bordering on pleasurable pain. Three long strides carried us around the bed, where he threw back the covers and laid me on my back in the middle of the queen-sized bed. One huge hand brushed a strand of hair away from my face and tucked it behind my ear.

Molten chocolate eyes met mine. "Thank you."

"For what?" I tipped my chin up to him, studying him, and he smiled.

"For loving me when you didn't have to."

"I guess my heart was right all along." A soft smile crossed my face and I pulled him down for a kiss. "I'll always love you."

"And I will always love you."

Still sheathed inside me, he was half-hard, and I could feel the remnants of our lovemaking leak out of me as he moved. The ramifications of what we'd just done—again— hit me with the force of a freight train.

Shit. He'd come inside me multiple times. Despite the fact that he said he loved me, there was so much unknown, and I couldn't help the fear and unease roiling in my belly. We hadn't talked about what the future would truly bring, and I needed to know. What would I do if I was pregnant? The possibility of having kids had seemed out of reach for so long now, I'd almost dismissed it. Would he be true to his word? Would he be there for me and our baby?

"Jack?" I hated that my voice shook under the strain of my worry.

He seemed to know exactly what I was asking, because one huge hand wrapped around the back of my neck and guided my gaze to his. "I will always take care of you, Mia."

"I just..." Why was this so hard to say? "What if...?"

Briefly his eyes dropped to my midsection before returning my pleading stare. "Do you want a baby?"

With him? "More than anything."

"You know what I want?" His question caught me off guard. Or maybe it was the intense look in his eyes that sent a flurry of worry and hope mingling in my belly. I shook my head, my brows furrowed, afraid to breathe. He studied me for a second before brushing his lips over mine in a sweet, whisper-soft caress. "What I want..." Two huge hands cradled my head as he stared down at me. "...is a little girl..." He kissed me between words. "...who's as beautiful... and strong... and sweet as you."

"Really?" It was the last thing I'd expected, and everything I needed to hear. Joyful tears burned my eyes.

Jack nodded. "Let's make it happen."

Our lips crashed together as I pulled his head down to mine, desperately needing the contact. I loved this man so much. I wanted more than anything to make his words come true. I would never get enough of him, and it seemed he wanted me just as badly.

As if to prove my point, his hips flexed, and the head of his cock bumped my cervix, causing me to cry out. Desire flared, ripping through my blood, and I lifted my hips to meet his. Warm lips brushed mine as he pulled out of my body almost to the tip. He drove into me so suddenly and so roughly that it stole my breath. My tits bounced under the force of his thrust, and his gaze dropped to my chest. Lowering his head, he captured one taut nipple in his mouth and suckled.

Lightning shot to my core, almost instantly pushing me to the edge. Teeth scraped over the sensitive flesh as he pulled out and drove home again, teasing my body mercilessly. Desire, raw and unrestrained, swept through me, and I dug my fingers into his back, urging him on.

Dimly, I was aware of a high-pitched tone to the right. My haze of desire lifted as I realized the strange sound was coming from the phone on the nightstand. It'd been so long since I'd heard the shrill ring of the old-style phones that I hadn't even recognized it at first.

I lifted my hands and gently pushed on Jack's chest. Reluctantly, he broke the kiss. "Do you want to get that?"

"Nope." Jack barely breathed the word before capturing my lips again, his tongue sweeping over mine.

The ringing pierced the air again, and I shoved against him, more insistently this time. "What if it's important?"

He shook his head, face only inches from mine. "Probably just our clothes. Not worried about it."

The phone rang again as his head lowered once more, and I turned toward the sound. "If you don't answer, they'll probably send someone up."

Jack froze for a millisecond as my statement registered. "Goddammit."

Agitation flickered in his dark gaze, and I pulled my lips into my mouth to refrain from smiling. One huge hand scooped under my butt, and I let out a soft cry as he lifted me, simultaneously shifting us closer to the edge of the bed, his cock still lodged firmly inside me.

He swiped at the contraption as it chirped out another ring, but his fingers brushed the receiver, knocking it off the nightstand and onto the floor instead.

"Motherfucker!"

I turned my mouth into my shoulder to stifle my laugh as Jack used the cord to drag the phone back up. He shot me a quick glare. "You think that's funny?"

A grin split my face. "A little."

Eyes on me, Jack lifted the receiver to his ear. "Yeah?" His dick pulled free of my channel, then slammed back in, and I tossed my head back, biting my lip so the person on the other end wouldn't hear my wanton cries.

"That's great, I'll be down to get them in a few." Staring down at me with an intense expression, he swiveled his hips, grinding against my clit and dragging me to the precipice of release once more. God, I would never get enough of this man. My body trembled, and I dug my heels into his butt, trying to rub against him. His nostrils flared and his eyes darkened. Tone hard, he spoke into the phone. "Okay, thanks."

Stretching to the side, he slammed the receiver down, then threaded his hand into my hair. "You're in so much trouble."

"Oh?" Was that breathy voice really mine? The thought dissipated as my walls constricted around his hard shaft.

"Yep." He nipped at my lower lip, then swept his

tongue over to soothe the sting. "You want a baby, you're gonna leave here carrying my child."

His words sent a thrill down my spine. "You sound pretty sure of yourself."

"I'm a man of my word." Jack rose to his knees, lifting my hips with him so only the tips of my toes remained on the bed. "I'm gonna do my best to make that happen."

His cock pulled free, only to slam back in, and my stomach muscles tightened under the strain of holding me up, but I couldn't deny the pleasure pulsing through me. One hand held my bottom secure while the other moved to my clit. His thumb pressed down on the sensitive nub, and I let out a moan as he plunged inside once more. My entire body quivered with need, and I gave over to it as my orgasm hit me with lightning speed.

Every thought fled my brain as he fucked me hard and fast. Less than a minute later he came with a guttural groan. Lowering our bodies to the bed, he braced himself over me, still breathing heavily. His mouth skated over my neck and collarbone, down to my chest, where he kissed the space right over my heart.

"Love you, Mia mine."

I wrapped my arms around his shoulders and held him close. "Forever."

TWENTY-FOUR

Jack

I watched Mia from across the room as she tore the tags off the new yoga pants and stepped into them. Every moment with her was like seeing her for the first time. I loved everything about her.

In my ear, Hailey spoke, her voice pitched low and soothing as if to comfort me. "Bella's doing wonderfully, Mr. Prescott. Dr. Carpenter gave her more medication to help with the pain but she's alert and doing well."

The words lifted a boulder of worry from my shoulders. "Thanks, Hailey. If anything changes, please call the hotel. We're in room 619."

I rattled off the number and hung up, then powered down my phone and tossed it aside. I'd left without anything this afternoon, including a phone charger. I called the vet's office to give them the number to the hotel, but I had an ulterior motive. I needed to know Bella was all right.

Mia tugged a sweatshirt over her head and met my gaze. "Everything okay?"

"Perfect." I grimaced. "I probably seem like an overprotective parent. I think Hailey was laughing at me."

Mia smiled and crossed over to where I sat on the edge of the bed. Resting her hands on my shoulders, she moved into the vee of my legs. "Nothing wrong with taking care of the ones you love."

Snaking my arms around her waist, I held her tightly, my face pressed against her chest. "I love you, Mia."

I couldn't stop saying it, but she didn't seem to mind. "Love you, too." She dropped a quick kiss on my mouth. "Are you hungry?"

My gaze raked over her breasts, just inches from my face. Not for food. "Starving."

"Good." She grabbed my hand and pulled me to my feet. "Let's go see what the vendors have to offer."

Hand in hand, we headed downstairs and meandered through the various booths, examining the crafts from local artists and food booths local restaurants had set up in the park. Mia paused next to a tent displaying dozens of black velvet jewelry stands, and I stepped up next to her. An older man greeted Mia with a gap-toothed smile. "Evenin', ma'am. Looking for anything in particular?"

"Just browsing," she demurred.

The man studied her intently before switching his gaze to me. "How long have you been together?"

Mia and I exchanged a look, and I offered him a partial truth. "It feels like forever."

And it did; it felt as though I'd known her my entire life, yet not nearly long enough. The one thing I did know, though, was that I wanted her by my side every day from now on.

The man smiled knowingly and gestured to the tray of

rings Mia was looking at. "Each gemstone has a meaning. Are you familiar?"

Mia shook her head. "I don't know much about jewels."

He smiled and slipped a jade ring from its slot. "Jade is said to bring wisdom and luck. In some cultures, it is believed to bless anything it touches."

Well, that was promising. I smiled indulgently as Mia fingered the pretty stone.

She handed the ring back to the man and continued to peruse the trays. He eyed her. "What is your birthstone?"

She glanced up with a smile. "Opal."

"Ah." His eyes lit up. "A stone with a most conflicting history."

"Why's that?" Mia asked as he handed her an opal ring.

"Many years ago, opals were believed to bring bad luck," the man began. "It was once associated with misfortune and death. But"—he held up a finger—"over the years people have come to appreciate the stone, and they say that it is a symbol of love and purity, and that it brings hope and happiness."

The rainbow of colors sparkled in the glow of the lights strung overhead, catching my eye. I turned the man's words over in my mind, and I couldn't help but think of our past. It seemed appropriate almost, with the demise of their marriage and our ability to overcome and persevere. Perhaps, like the feelings the stone was reputed to foster, we could find happiness despite the odds.

"We'll take it."

Mia's head whipped toward mine. "Are you sure?"

I nodded. I'd never been more sure of anything in my life. With a smile, she slipped it on her hand—her right hand, I noticed—as I handed over several bills.

Mia looped one arm through mine, and I glanced down

at her. A soft smile on her pretty face, she looked happy. I tugged her to a stop.

"What's—?"

Before she could finish the thought, I slanted my mouth over hers. The kiss went on endlessly before I pulled back and gazed into those gorgeous turquoise eyes I'd missed so much. "I love you, that's all."

Her face softened, practically melting. "Forever."

Slipping my hand into hers, I turned abruptly and headed for the hotel, pulling her behind me. Her laugh reached my ears, bringing a smile to my face. Every emotion was a direct reflection of Mia herself. Her happiness made me happy; I was desolate when she was sad.

Yanking the key card out of my back pocket, I shoved it into the black box on the hotel door and waited impatiently for the telltale beep to grant us entrance. As soon as the lock disengaged, I shoved the handle and flung the door wide, dragging Mia inside. Pressing her up against the wall in the hallway, I took her mouth in a brutal kiss, trapping her body with mine. She responded eagerly, twining her arms around my neck and giving as good as she got.

Scooping her into my arms, I carried her back to the bed. Thirty seconds later, we were both bare and I used my large frame to press her lithe body in the mattress.

"Mia?"

"Yeah?" Her voice was soft and breathy, and I loved that I'd done that to her.

"What do you say to starting over?"

Twin lines marred the skin between her eyes as confusion reigned. "What do you mean?"

"I was so unhappy for so long without you. You're the only thing that's ever mattered," I began. "When we split..."

I shook my head, because that was wrong. "I screwed up. I should have talked to you first before reenlisting."

She opened her mouth to speak, but I placed a finger over her lips, stealing the words. "Please. Just let me get this out." I took a deep breath. "I never once thought about how it would affect you emotionally. I thought I was doing what was best for you—but I was wrong. I don't ever want something like that to come between us again. I promise, Mia. If you give me this chance, I'll do my damnedest to make you proud."

"Jack." Tears filled her eyes. "I've always been proud of you. So much, you have no idea. And I never stopped loving you. We both made mistakes. We both said things we didn't mean back then."

"I was your first kiss, Mia." I lifted her right hand and kissed her fingertips before easing the ring over her knuckle. "And I want to be your last."

I held my breath, waiting for her to connect the dots. "Jack...?"

Grabbing her left hand, I slipped the ring onto her third finger. "Will you marry me?" I waited a beat. "Again?"

"Yes." My heart leaped as she flung her arms around my neck. "Yes!"

Our mouths met in a hard collision. Her plump lips parted, and I swept my tongue inside, tangling it with hers. She tasted of apple cider and everything undeniably Mia. I fucking loved it. Over and over, I plunged inside her mouth while my hands roamed every curve of her body. My right hand cupped the swell of her breast, and she let out a low moan as my thumb swept over the hardened peak.

Nipping her bottom lip, I rolled her nipple between my thumb and forefinger, and her hips jumped off the bed at the sensation. One kiss bled into another, each growing slightly less frantic and more tender. Settling myself in the cradle of her hips, I slowly slid inside her, reveling in the way she fit me so perfectly. Instead of the primal sex we'd shared earlier, this time it was infinitely more sensual, as if we finally understood that the other wasn't going anywhere. This time, I showed her the attention she deserved. I took her slowly, making love to her—making her mine again.

TWENTY-FIVE

Mia

The past day and a half seemed like a dream. No—more like a nightmare.

Jack stroked my shoulder with his thumb as if to remind me of his presence. Like I could forget. I wanted to forget everything of the past twenty-four hours, rewind time so none of it had ever happened.

Maybe not all of it. I twisted the ring on my finger and shot a quick glance at Jack out of the corner of my eyes. I wouldn't trade our time together for anything. He was everything I've ever wanted and more. We'd been through hell on earth, but I was sure that, whatever the future brought, we would get through it together. We were strong —better—together.

With a deep breath, I started from the beginning. "When he said he was the last person to see my dad—"

My voice broke, and Jack rubbed my shoulder. "It's okay, honey."

I shook my head. I needed to know. I glanced at Eric. "Did he...?"

"I don't know anything for sure, but..." His face contorted in a grimace. "I called the facility your father was in, and they verified that both Janine and Kenneth were present the day your father passed away."

Tears burned my eyes. Why would they do something so horrible? I couldn't figure it out. Jack pulled me further into his embrace, and I buried my head against his chest. His voice rumbled up as he spoke with the sheriff. "I think we're done here."

Eric's rough voice cut in. "I have your statements. You're free—"

"No." I pushed away from him and swiped at my eyes. Both men studied me, and my gaze darted between them. "I'm fine, really."

First thing this morning, we'd stopped at the vet's office in Kalispell to check on Bella. She was still in pain, but she seemed to be okay considering everything that had happened. I still blamed myself for her injuries. Had I turned Kenneth away, maybe it never would have happened. I knew what Jack had said was true, though—If Kenneth hadn't cornered me at the cabin, he would've found another way. And maybe we wouldn't have been as lucky that time.

Jack sat next to me, one arm draped over the back of my chair, lending silent strength as I stared across the desk at Donahue.

"What happens now?"

Eric studied me. "I'll be taking Janine down to the county jail this afternoon, where they'll begin the arraignment process."

My body stiffened. *She's still here?* Part of me wanted to cower and hide. The other part of me wanted to jump from my seat and confront her. I wanted to ask her why. Why had they hurt so many people? And I couldn't help the rage bubbling up inside me. I hated her. She and Kenneth had taken so much away from me—from us. Without Eric and Jack to stop them, who knew how many lives they would've taken? And all because of greed. Had Janine been kind and civil, I probably would've contemplated selling off my portion of the business. But they'd clearly had this plan in place long before Dad got sick. The thought pissed me off all over again.

Jack seemed to know what I was thinking, because his mouth brushed my ear as he spoke. "She's not worth it. It's over and you're safe now; that's all that matters."

Sheriff Donahue offered me a small smile. "I'll do everything I can to put her away for good."

It wasn't nearly enough, not after everything that had happened. Although I still wasn't quite ready to let go of my anger toward my stepmother, I nodded anyway.

Jack stood, pulling me with him, and stretched one hand across the desk. "Thanks again. And if you need anything else, just give me a call."

"Will do." Eric returned the handshake. His next words were directed to me as his gaze fell meaningfully to the ring on my left hand. "Good luck."

Jack and I made the trip to the cabin in relative silence. In all honesty, I was dreading coming back here, but I needed to face my demons. I needed closure from the past few days before I could move on. Jack had asked me to move into his place for our remaining time here, and I'd happily agreed. I wanted to spend time getting to know each other—

for real this time. No secrets, no holding back. Just the two of us making it work.

My agitation increased the closer we got to Dad's cabin. All I could see was Bella lying in a pool of her own blood, Kenneth's dark, hateful gaze on me as he forced his way inside. Silently, Jack slid his hand over the console toward me, palm up. I glanced at it for a long moment before twining my fingers through his. His love and reassurance seeped into my soul, and I knew everything was going to be okay. Maybe not today, maybe not right away, but as long as Jack was by my side, I knew we could overcome anything life threw our way.

My chest constricted as Jack turned into the driveway and slowed to a stop in front of the cabin. With one last silent squeeze of my fingers, he helped me out of the truck and guided me inside, his palm firm and warm on the small of my back.

Once inside, I glanced around. It was strange being back here. A shiver wracked my body, and not because of the cold. Blood still stained the floor in the hallway, and I burrowed into Jack's embrace as he slid one arm around my shoulders, the other wrapping around my waist. Tears burned my eyes and blurred my vision as they trickled down my cheeks.

I couldn't dispel the regret and grief swamping me. As if reading my thoughts, Jack shifted me in his arms and cupped my face with one huge palm. He brushed away a stray tear with the gentlest of touches and met my gaze. "Everything is going to be fine, baby. You're safe, and Bella's gonna be okay. That's all that matters."

I nodded and wedged one hand between us to swipe at my tears. "I know, but—"

"No buts." He shook his head. "What's done is done. From here on out, we'll move on—together."

A pounding on the door made me jump. As if acting on instinct, Jack thrust me behind him, putting himself between me and whoever was on the other side of the door.

"Amelia!"

My racing heart calmed a bit at the sound of Brent's voice, and I laid one hand on Jack's shoulder. "It's Brent."

"I know." Lips pressed into a flat line, he threw a glance over his shoulder at me. "Do you want to see him?"

Did I? I still wasn't sure how involved he was in this whole scheme, if at all. I bit my lip, my gaze darting between Jack and the front door. Before everything had happened, I'd planned to confront him. I needed to at least hear what he had to say. With Jack here, I knew I had nothing to worry about.

Slowly, I nodded. "Let him in."

Jack strode to the door and opened it. I couldn't hear the words he spoke to Brent, but my stepbrother pushed past him, and Jack closed the door with a growl.

"God, Amelia." His feet ate up the distance between us. I flinched as he threw his arms around me in a hard hug. A second later, his body was ripped away from mine, Jack's huge hand planted in Brent's solar plexus.

"Don't fucking touch her."

Relief and guilt warred within me. Brent's expression spoke of hurt and confusion as he glanced between me and Jack. "It's fine, Jack."

Flicking a quick look at me to ascertain my admission, he turned his glower back on Brent and finally dropped his hand away. "Fine."

Brent stared at me, and I swore I could see moisture in his eyes. "You're really okay?" I nodded, and he let out a relieved breath. "Thank God. When they said…" He dropped his gaze to the floor, his voice a broken whisper. "I didn't know what to think."

I met Jack's eyes. "Can you give us a second?"

Every muscle tensed as if he were physically restraining himself. "Are you sure?"

"I'm sure." I leaned up and grazed my lips across his jaw. "Would you mind making me some tea?"

One arm slipped around my waist, and he squeezed gently before dropping a soft kiss on my mouth. "Of course."

He threw a warning look at Brent before pushing past him toward the kitchen. I saw Brent shudder as his eyes landed on the blood marring the hallway, and his face went white. I threaded my arm through his. "Come on."

He reluctantly fell into step beside me, and we crossed to the living room. I curled into the end of the couch while he sank into the armchair just a few feet away. I felt Jack's eyes on me as he moved around the kitchen, and it filled me with warmth.

Brent studied me for a second, watching me watch Jack. I met his eyes and he offered a small smile. "Are you happy?"

I nodded. "I am. He's…" I couldn't come up with a word that accurately described how I felt about Jack. He was my everything.

Brent nodded as if he understood. "Good." Silence fell for a moment before he spoke again. "I'm so sorry about everything. If I'd known…"

He trailed off, and I pierced him with a questioning gaze. I knew Jack believed him innocent, but I had to know for myself. "Did you have anything to do with it?"

He blew out a harsh breath, his expression wounded. "I deserve that. But no. I didn't know."

I studied him, examining his sincerity. "How did you know we were here?"

Brent smiled sheepishly. "I was in Pine Ridge when I saw Jack drive past. I needed to talk to you, so I followed you guys here."

I couldn't tell if what he said was true or not. Honestly, I didn't know if I'd trust him ever again. The thought brought me up short. Brent was my stepbrother—the one person who'd been there for me when no one else had. Didn't he deserve the benefit of the doubt? I was doing to him exactly what I'd done to Jack, shutting him out before he even had a chance to defend himself.

I stared at him, his eyes filled with a combination of remorse and hope for reconciliation. "Okay." I nodded, twisting the ring around my finger.

The motion caught Brent's attention, and his brows jumped to his hairline. "Is that...?"

I followed his gaze to where my hand twisted in my lap. "It is."

His expression softened. "I'm happy for you, sis."

"Thanks." Brent and Jack had never been close, so I knew how much it took for him to accept my happiness with the man who'd broken my heart. Brent had seen me at my lowest point, completely broken after my divorce. What he still didn't know, though, was that I'd been the one at fault. I hadn't yet had a chance to explain everything, but that was a conversation for another day.

My attention was drawn to Jack as he slipped between the sofa and coffee table. He passed me a steaming mug before settling on the cushion beside me and looping a strong arm around my shoulders. Chocolate eyes searched mine. "You good?"

I wrapped my hands around the warm mug, absorbing its warmth. Despite everything from the past few days, I couldn't help but count my blessings. I was surrounded by love from the two people closest to me. A smile lifted my mouth as my gaze darted between the two of them. "I'm perfect."

EPILOGUE

Jack

ONE MONTH LATER

Light spilled in through the huge windows, illuminating my wife in a halo of ethereal light.

My wife.

Almost.

"You may kiss the bride."

A huge grin cracked my face at the preacher's words, and I wrapped one hand around Mia's neck. "Love you, Mia mine."

Sparkling blue eyes glistened with unshed tears. "Love you forever."

Hoots and hollers filled the air as my lips crashed against hers. I pulled back a fraction of an inch and pressed my forehead to hers, meeting her gaze. "Forever."

A radiant smile lit her face, and I couldn't help but steal another kiss. I'd never take her for granted again. Releasing her, I turned to our closest family and friends. Brent and Carter sat in the front row, surrounded by the rest of our crew and a few select friends we'd invited to Briarleigh.

A month ago, I never would have envisioned being this happy ever again. I'd been broken and empty, missing a huge part of me. But now that hole in my heart was filled, and with Mia by my side, I knew everything was going to be okay. I looped one arm around her waist and addressed our friends. "Thank you all for being a part of this. I can't begin to tell you how much we appreciate your support. We'd love for you to join us in the great room for food and cake."

Everyone had approved wholeheartedly, even Brent. We still weren't the best of friends, but we made it work for Mia's sake. He'd taken a week off work to come up for our wedding, and I knew it had pleased Mia immensely. He was her only remaining family, besides me, and I knew how important it was to her to stay in touch with him.

She'd wanted to keep the house on Briarleigh, but I'd talked her into selling it. It held so many memories, both good and bad, and I thought we needed a fresh start. She immediately jumped on board when we started talking about building our own house, complete with a studio for her photography.

I knew she'd never want to give it up, though she'd decided she wanted to contribute to Hamilton Construction as well. Over the past few weeks, she'd taken shots of Briarleigh from every angle imaginable—even the damn helicopter that Carter had rented. The stupid shit had heliskied down the mountain just as he'd planned, and Mia had insisted on riding along. I wasn't about to leave her alone with him, so we took a tour of the area, flying over the resort and surrounding mountains.

We'd timed the wedding well, wanting to get it in before the crew left. The soft opening was only a week away, and everything had fallen neatly into place. I didn't know what Eric had said to Toby, but the man seemed to have pulled his head out of his ass. He'd come around a couple weeks back to apologize personally—to both me and Mia—and he'd even asked about picking up some work around the lodge. I'd been more than a little concerned, but Mia convinced me to give him a shot. And I was glad I had. He'd more than proved himself recently, recruiting more residents of Pine Ridge.

Mia glanced around the huge room once more. We'd decorated the rec room off the hotel lobby for our wedding, turning it into an indoor winter wonderland. Sparkling white lights hung from the rafters, and trees decorated with bows and shiny ornaments filled each corner, adding to the ambiance. "Have you thought about what to do with this room?"

A predatory smile curved my mouth, and I took my wife in my arms. "Shouldn't we at least wait for the guests to leave?"

It took only a second for my implication to sink in, and she slapped a palm against my chest. "No! That's not..." Her cheeks burned red, making me love her all the more. "*Anyway...*"

Unable to keep from touching her, I cradled her jaw and tipped her mouth up to meet mine. I took my time exploring her lips, the soft, berry-red flesh like the sweetest wine. It was over much too soon, and she leaned away from me with a hushed whisper. "Someone will see!"

I rolled my eyes. "That's the point. We're married, they understand."

"I—" She paused and pressed a hand to her stomach. "I'll be right back."

She started to turn away, but I caught her elbow and swung her back to me. My brows drew together as my gaze swept over her pale face. "Are you feeling okay?"

She waved away my concern. "I'll be fine."

With one last unconvincing smile, she pulled away and I watched as she headed to the bathroom. I swore she'd gone just before the ceremony, which had only been—I checked my watch—less than half an hour ago. She'd looked a little green then too, and I hoped she wasn't coming down with whatever had spread through the crew like wildfire last month. I'd never been so sick in my life.

Sheriff Donahue moved to my side and shook my hand, pulling my attention from Mia. "Congratulations."

"Thank you. I owe you one."

We'd never spoken of it, but I truly did. His words to me that day had meant the world. Without his encouragement, I may never have tried to fix things. He nodded, as if he understood completely.

He knelt and scratched Bella behind the ears. Her tongue lolled happily under the attention, her eyes closing in ecstasy as she flopped to the side on the huge memory foam doggie bed, offering her belly up for a rub. Eric chuckled and obliged before pushing to his feet. "How's she doing?"

"Good. Moving a little slow, still, but that's to be expected." We'd had another checkup with Dr. Carpenter earlier this week, who'd pronounced her healthy and recovering well. "She doesn't want to leave Mia's side."

"Can't blame her." He scanned the room, and I watched

his posture change as his eyes locked in on whatever—or whoever—he'd been looking for. "Jules fitting in okay?"

Eric's voice was quiet, for my ears only, and I followed his gaze to the beautiful, reserved brunette across the room. No explanation, he'd approached me a couple weeks ago and asked if Jules could work at the resort. I had no idea how she'd ended up at his place, but I figured it was the least I could do for her.

She rarely smiled and she avoided people—especially men—like the plague. The only exception to this seemed to be Eric himself. He dropped her off and picked her up each day, and I paid her right before she left—in cash. She barely looked me in the eye and kept a healthy distance between us. I didn't know what or who she was running from, but I knew there was more to the story. Whatever the situation was, it wasn't good. "She's a hard worker. Mostly keeps to herself."

He nodded. "She's a good girl."

He watched her like a hawk, and I couldn't help but wonder if there was more to it than just concern on his part. I recognized that look—it was the same thing I felt each time I saw my wife.

As if my thoughts conjured her, Mia glided toward us, a huge smile on her face. She greeted Eric with a friendly hug, and a spark of envy shot through me. I was never going to like seeing another man's hands on my wife, even if they belonged to a close friend.

He returned the hug, if a bit awkwardly, and smiled down at her. "You're going to have your hands full with this one."

"Oh, I know it." She threw me a saucy wink, and I wrapped one arm around her waist, pulling her close.

Eric glanced between the two of us before his attention

was drawn once more across the room. With a distracted nod and a final murmured "congratulations," he headed toward Jules.

Mia watched as he approached the brunette, and Jules smiled shyly as Eric moved protectively to her side. "I like her. I hope she sticks around."

I trusted what Eric had said. The girl was meek, and I knew there was more to the story, but if he said we didn't have anything to worry about, then I'd take his word for it. I hummed a noncommittal sound, not really caring one way or the other whether the girl stayed or left. "Why's that?"

"She'd make a great babysitter."

Concern for the sheriff forgotten, my eyes narrowed on my wife. "I'm sorry?"

"You should be." She nodded perfunctorily before meeting my gaze.

I shifted so she faced me fully and studied her face. "Explain."

"Really?" She rolled her eyes. "This was your plan, if you recall. That night we spent at the hotel in Kalispell…" She trailed off, and my pulsed leaped.

"What exactly are you telling me?"

"I go to the bathroom twelve times a day. My boobs are bigger. Don't tell me you didn't notice," she teased.

I had, but I didn't say anything. My gaze dropped to her flat belly before jumping back to her face. "Really?"

"Really." Her megawatt smile lit her eyes, filling them with warmth and happiness. "You're gonna be a daddy."

"Fuck, baby." Wrapping one hand around the back of her neck, I pulled her to me, securing my other arm around her waist. I held her tightly, my head burrowed against the sleek slope of her neck as a myriad of emotions crashed over me. Gratitude. Fear. But mostly love.

I lifted my head to meet her gaze and cradled her jaw in my hand. Emotion clogged my throat, turning my voice raspy. "Thank you."

She shook her head, and a tear spilled down her cheek. "We deserve this."

Yes, we did. After everything we'd been through, we both deserved something good. Our tangled past was messy and complicated and painful at times. But each moment, every mistake we'd made, had brought us here, together—and I wouldn't trade it for the world.

If you loved Jack and Mia's story, you won't want to miss the next book in the Retribution Series! On the run from her abusive uncle, Jules has finally found a safe haven in Pine Ridge... But when someone makes it clear they're out for revenge, Sheriff Eric Donahue is the only one who can protect her. Turn the page for your first look at Pretty Little Lies!

PRETTY LITTLE LIES

Giuliana

The first footfall made my heart beat double-time, and I inhaled deeply, trying to slow its rapid pace.

Thump-thump. Thump-thump.

Two hours.

Seven thousand, two hundred beats.

Once, I'd counted each and every one. But the higher I counted, the more anxious I became. I clenched my eyes closed tighter and drew in a deep, calming breath, trying to bring the sights and sounds of the beach back into focus. I could feel the heat of the sun on my skin, the shifting of the grains of sand as I pulled my knees more tightly to my chest. A slight breeze blew in over the ocean, whipping strands of hair across my face, and waves lapped gently at the shore, bringing with them the salty scent of the ocean.

The vibration of another footstep against the hard floor ripped me from my reverie, and I tightened my hold on my legs. The footsteps drew closer, and I reluctantly opened my eyes. Darkness pressed in around me, and my heart kicked into overdrive as my chest rose and fell on shallow, uneven breaths. The air inside the tiny closet felt thick and hot, making it hard to breathe.

The door suddenly flew open, and I blinked against the rectangle of light. My uncle's form was outlined in the garish glow, and I forced myself not to flinch away from him. I wished I could physically retreat to my beach as I'd done in my daydreams. It'd become a coping mechanism for me, much like soldiers or agents who used such mental tactics when captured and tortured.

"Get up."

My knees ached as I unfolded myself from the floor. It took a moment for the blood to resume flowing normally after hours of being cramped up, and I felt a bit light-headed as I leaned one shoulder against the wall. The closet was my uncle's favorite form of abuse; he knew how much I hated dark, enclosed spaces. It wasn't the first time he'd punished me this way—but it would be the last. All because I'd asked to leave the house.

Uncle Massimo's face twisted into a sneer, and he spun on a heel as if disgusted by the sight of me. My heart clenched in my chest, knowing that it was probably true, though I was unsure exactly why he felt that way. I tried so hard to blend into the background, to avoid drawing attention to myself, but I never seemed to escape his notice.

I wiped my clammy hands on my skirt before straightening my shoulders and stepping into his office. My uncle sat behind the wide cherry desk, his expression unreadable as I closed the closet door behind me and turned to face him. No one ever spoke without my uncle's permission. We stared at each other for a long moment, and my fingers twitched at my sides. It was a nervous tic I couldn't control, and one that I knew my uncle hated most of all. I'd started picking at my nails soon after my father's death, and it irked my uncle to no end.

I was, at all times, supposed to be a poised, perfect porcelain doll. Uncle resented me for being the only child of his brother, former capo of the Capaldi family, and I knew his plan was to marry me off. I should've been married nearly two years ago, but thanks to my cousin Matteo's pleading, Uncle agreed to push the wedding back to my twentieth birthday. I had hoped it would be someone in the *famiglia* that I was comfortable with, at least.

Unfortunately, that wasn't the case. My birthday was a little over a week away, and Uncle Massimo had arranged my betrothal to Nikolai, a member of the Russian Bratva. The fighting had escalated after Daddy's death, the death toll climbing each week until Massimo struck a deal with their captain. Nikolai needed a wife; I was to fill that role.

Our marriage was intended to strengthen the bonds between the two families and settle the unrest. That was all fine and good for the others—but what about me? Nikolai was notoriously cruel, and I'd heard stories that made my stomach turn. Matteo said he'd been married twice before. Both women had mysteriously disappeared and, as far as I knew, they'd never been seen or heard from again. I pleaded for my uncle to reconsider, but my efforts were rewarded with two hours spent in the dark, cramped closet I'd just exited.

I barely repressed a shudder. I hated the closet—but I hated the idea of marrying an abusive man more. A white gown hung in my room, just waiting for me to put it on and walk down the aisle for my big day—a day I vowed would never happen.

Uncle met my gaze and lifted a well-manicured dark eyebrow. "Well?"

I swallowed down my unease, once more asking the question I'd dared to bring up more than two hours ago. "I wish to go to the mall today."

Uncle stared at me for a moment. "Weren't you just there last week? I seem to remember you spending nearly three hundred dollars last time."

Three hundred dollars of my money. Though I had technically inherited everything after my father passed, my uncle had taken it upon himself to act as my advisor. What that truly meant was that he owned me. He kept me confined to the house, not allowing me interaction with anyone, not even my own mother. On the rare occasion that I was allowed to leave the house, it was under the intense scrutiny of at least two guards.

He said it was for my safety; I knew better. He wanted to keep me away from everyone—especially anyone who might be able to overthrow his complete and total power over me. Once he married me off, the money that was rightfully mine would go to my new husband— half of it, at least. It was part of the deal that Massimo had struck with Nikolai. I'd be damned if I would be traded like chattel.

Refusing to back down, I pled my case. "It's for my fashion blog," I started, and he let out a stifled noise.

He waved one hand in the air. "Isn't it about time you grow up and give that thing up? No one cares about it anyway."

I bit my tongue at the slight. I actually did have several hundred followers, but he was right about one thing—I didn't care about the blog in the least. It was a front, a necessary evil, and something I had to stick to for the time being. "Please, Uncle," I requested.

"No." He picked up his pen again and began to write,

the decisive action signaling the end of our conversation. Desperation crawled up my throat.

"Uncle," I started, then immediately snapped my mouth closed. His cold, dark eyes snapped to mine, and the set of his shoulders told me I'd made a grave mistake. Slowly, he stood from his chair and rounded the desk. His gaze never strayed from mine, and my legs trembled with the urge to run. My heart raced wildly in my chest as each step brought him closer until he was barely a foot away.

"Why must you always learn the hard way, Giuliana?"

I swallowed down the hatred filling me and bit off the response that jumped to the tip of my tongue. Curling my hand into a fist at my side, I dug the nail of my index finger into my thumb. The slight pain helped to ground me.

Unfortunately, my uncle did not miss the movement. With lightning fast speed, he snatched up my wrist and brought it between us. Unfurling my hand, he examined my nails, and a sneer marred his handsome features. "Have you been biting your nails again?"

My hand shook where he held it, and I stumbled over my words. "I... I've been trying not to, Uncle." His grip tightened on my wrist, and I knew I would have bruises from those long fingers pressed against my skin.

"Haven't I told you how much I despise that habit?"

"I'm sorry—" I started, but he cut over me.

"How do you expect a man like Nikolai to marry you when you look so filthy all the time?"

The sharp barb sent a pain through my chest, but I refused to rise to his bait.

"I asked you a question!" In a move that took my breath away, Uncle released my hands and gripped my biceps. With a hard shove, he slammed me against the wall. A spark of pain shot through my head, sending a shower of black spots swirling before my eyes. Before I could recover and even contemplate formulating a response, he released me, throwing me to the side and off-balance. I stumbled and fell, unable to get my hands in front of me in time. My head struck the sideboard on the way down, and pain shot through me as I crumpled to the floor.

Uncle Massimo pressed a polished Italian loafer to my throat, and I clawed at his leg, trying to get him to release me. My lungs burned and my throat ached as he slowly cut off the oxygen. Finally he stepped away and shook his head. "Worthless."

I scrambled away, clutching my throat and pressing my back to the wall, putting as much distance between us as possible. I didn't know why he hated me so much, but I knew that, despite his tendency to hurt me, he would never kill me. I was worth much more to him alive.

He shoved his hands in the pockets of his trousers and adopted a casual pose before speaking. "You may go. Be sure to get a dress for your engagement party."

My mind muddled, I managed to choke out the words, "Engagement party?"

"That's right." A snake-like smile curved his mouth. "Nikolai will be here for dinner after mass on Sunday. You'll want to make a good impression."

"B-but—"

With one swift move, my uncle closed the distance between us and wrapped a hand around my aching throat. He lifted me to my feet and slammed my back against the wall. "Your sacrifice will unite us with the Russians. There has been much unrest, and your marriage will be seen as a peace offering. We've been at odds too long. You are the key to our success." He released me and stepped away.

Fury burned through me, and I longed to scream at him.

Biting my tongue, I dipped my head in a portrait of submission. It would do no good to argue with him. A long moment later, I flinched as his hand moved under my chin and directed my gaze to his.

"Clean yourself up before you go. And get a manicure while you're out. Your nails look disgusting."

I lifted my chin. "I'd planned to..., sir."

His dark eyes flared at the inflection—and complete lack of respect—in that last word. His thumb and forefinger tightened on my chin. "One of these days, Giuliana, you will push too far. Perhaps Nikolai will teach you some manners."

With that last parting shot, he thrust my chin away from him and strode back to his desk. Without another look at me, he settled into his chair and resumed his work.

I used the opportunity to silently slip out of the office before I let any tears fall. I hurt all over, my pride included, but I refused to let him see me cry. I wouldn't show weakness. Head held high, I made my way past the guards stationed at the office door and started toward my room. Matteo stepped out of the shadows and grabbed my wrist, pulling me to a halt. Skin still tender, I yanked my hand out of his grasp and massaged the sore flesh.

My cousin's eyebrows drew together, and he gingerly touched my hand. "What happened?"

The same thing that always happens.

I shook my head. "It's nothing."

Anger replaced his concern. "Did he hurt you?"

"Please don't say anything," I begged. It would just make it worse for both of us if Matteo put himself in the middle.

Matteo let out a hiss. "That bastard. I should kill him."

Neither of us were exempt from my uncle's cruel

actions, and I knew Matteo would be punished worse if he stood up in my defense. I placed a hand on his shoulder. "My birthday is next week."

"Like I could forget," my cousin replied bitterly. "Did he say anything about it?"

I nodded. "Y-yes." I shakily drew a shuddering breath. "My engagement party is this Sunday."

Matteo's eyes flared wide before sympathy infused the dark brown deaths. He pulled me into a hug and spoke next to my ear. "Oh, *principessa*. I would stop it if I could."

His hold was too tight, and his sympathy nearly broke me. I eased out of his hold. "Everything will be fine," I promised. At least, I hoped that was the case.

Back in my room, I selected a large handbag and shoved the clothes I'd purchased last week into the very bottom before covering them with a magazine then draping a chic, decorative scarf over the side. I didn't want to stuff it too full and draw any attention to it, so I only selected the most expensive items. A knot had begun to form on my forehead from where I'd struck the sideboard, and I brushed my bangs to one side to cover it.

Johnny and Tommy fell into step beside me as I approached the front door and walked to the car. My leg bounced nervously the whole drive, and I finally let out a small sigh of relief when we reached the small boutique. The owner, Lila, smiled at me as we entered. She was the one person I could count on to always brighten my day, and I returned her heartfelt smile. She greeted me with a hug, and we immediately began to select items from the racks. Blatantly ignoring the two bodyguards lurking by the front door, Lila and I made small talk as we searched. I spoke loudly and exuberantly about what I'd planned for this week's blog, hoping the men would tune me out.

Lila tossed a couple new items over her arm. "Let's try these first and see what you think."

Casting a look out of the corner of my eye at Tommy, I followed her to a dressing room in the back of the store. Lila entered first and hung up the clothes then turned to me as I entered. Her lips pressed into a firm line as she glanced at my forehead. She gave a slight shake of her head but didn't say a word; she just held out her hand and waited for me to retrieve the clothes I'd shoved into the bottom of my bag.

"Thank you for doing this," I whispered to her.

With an abrupt nod, she exited the dressing room and moved behind the counter, taking the items with her. I let out a deep breath as I closed the curtain behind her. *One step closer.*

I took my time trying on the clothes, not wanting to draw any attention to myself. Lila spoke to me through the curtain as I changed, and I stepped out to view myself in the three-way mirror when I was done. We examined the outfit for a moment, and I let Lila take a few pictures for my blog before deciding it was time for the next ensemble.

"Can you help unzip me?" I asked, just loudly enough for the men to hear.

"Of course," she replied, stepping into the dressing room behind me and closing the curtain. Lila unzipped the dress, and I turned around to face her. She held out several bills and I smiled gratefully as I slipped them from her fingers.

"You have no idea how much I appreciate this."

"There's a bag of clothes in the back hallway," she whispered. "Nothing fancy, just the basics to get you through," she said.

Impulsively, I pulled her into a tight hug. "Thank you so much."

"I'll miss you," she said, her eyes shiny with tears.

"Someday, I promise I'll repay you," I said.

She waved off my concern. "Just be safe."

With one last quick hug, she was gone, and I knew it was the last time I would ever see her. I listened for a moment as Lila kicked up conversation with Tommy. I quickly changed into the nondescript yoga pants and long-sleeved shirt she'd left for me and grabbed my bag. Leaving my heels behind, I slipped into the ballet flats I'd stowed in my purse. Sliding the curtain to one side, I peeked out. Johnny was staring at his cell phone, one foot crossed over the other as he leaned against the wall near the entrance of the store. Tommy was turned slightly away from me as he flirted with Lila.

Taking a deep breath, I slunk out of the dressing room and angled toward the back door. The knob turned easily under my fingertips, and I pushed it open just far enough for me to slide through, then closed it quietly behind me. The door exited into a dimly lit service hallway used for deliveries and for Lila to come and go each day. Trying not to rustle the bag, I scooped up the clothes that Lila had left for me and sent up one more silent thank you. Moving silently but quickly down the hallway, I exited into the back parking lot, keeping my head low.

I glanced around and found the car I was looking for. Lila's boyfriend had arranged the purchase of the small blue Cavalier and had left it in the back of the parking lot for me. I forced myself not to run even though my heart beat wildly, sure that I would be caught at any moment. I opened the rear door and tossed the clothes inside, along with my purse, before climbing into the driver seat. I closed and locked the door, then fished around under the floormat for the key. Shoving it into the ignition, I waited a heart-stopping second for the engine to turn over. As soon as it caught, I shifted into gear and pulled slowly out of the parking lot. Knuckles white, I curled my fingers around the steering wheel and turned onto the main drag.

Two hundred miles later, I finally stopped glancing in the rearview mirror. I had no idea where I was going, but it didn't matter. I was free.

Don't miss Pretty Little Lies, now available everywhere!

ALSO BY MORGAN JAMES

Quentin Security Series

Twisted Devil – Jason and Chloe

The Devil You Know – Blake and Victoria

Devil in the Details – Xander and Lydia

Devil in Disguise – Gavin and Kate

Heart of a Devil – Vince and Jana

Tempting the Devil – Clay and Abby

Devilish Intent – Con and Grace

Quentin Security Box Set One (Books 1-3)

Quentin Security Box Set Two (Books 4-6)

*Each book is a standalone within the series

Rescue & Redemption Series

Friendly Fire – Grayson and Claire

Cruel Vendetta – Drew and Emery

Silent Treatment – Finn and Harper

Reckless Pursuit – Aiden and Izzy

Dangerous Desires – Vaughn and Sienna

Cold Justice – Nick and Eden

Rescue & Redemption Box Set One (books 1-3)

Retribution Series

Standalones

Bad Billionaires

ABOUT THE AUTHOR

Morgan James is a USA Today bestselling author of contemporary and romantic suspense novels. She spent most of her childhood with her nose buried in a book, and she loves all things romantic, dark, and dirty. She currently resides in Ohio and is living happily ever after with her own alpha hero and their two kids.

Keep up with Morgan and stay up to date on sales, giveaways, and new releases:

Website | Facebook | Instagram | BookBub | Goodreads

Made in the USA
Coppell, TX
03 June 2024

33069286R00111